THE WOMEN OF BREWSTER PLACE

GLORIA NAYLOR

A Methuen Paperback

A Methuen Paperback

THE WOMEN OF BREWSTER PLACE

British Library Cataloguing in Publication Data

Naylor, Gloria
  The women of Brewster Place.
  I. Title
  813'.54[F]   PS3564.A895
  ISBN 0-413-14010-5

First published in Great Britain 1983 by Hodder and Stoughton Ltd
This edition published 1987 by Methuen London Ltd
11 New Fetter Lane, London EC4P 4EE
Copyright © 1980, 82 by Gloria Naylor

A portion of this book appeared originally in *Essence* magazine.

Grateful acknowledgement is made to the following
for permission to reprint copyrighted material:

Alfred A. Knopf, Inc., and Harold Ober Associates:
"What Happens to a Dream Deferred?"
from *The Panther and the Lash* by Langston Hughes.
Copyright © 1951 by Langston Hughes.

Edward B. Marks Music Corporation: Portions of
lyrics from "Strange Fruit" by Lewis Allan,
"Billie's Blues" by Billie Holiday, and
"God Bless the Child" by Arthur Herzog and Billie Holiday.
Copyright © Edward B. Marks Music Corporation. Used by permission.

MCA Music and ATV: A selection from
"Tain't Nobody's Biz-Ness If I Do," words and music
by Porter Grainger and Everett Robbins.
Copyright © 1922 by MCA Music, A Division of
MCA Inc, New York, NY. Copyright renewed.
Used by permission. All rights reserved.

Woodrow Music, Inc.: Selections from "Detour Ahead,"
words and music by Herb Ellis, John Frigo,
and Lou Carter. All rights reserved.

Printed in Great Britain by Richard Clay Ltd, Bungay, Suffolk

For
Marcia, who gave me the dream
Lauren, who believed in it
Rick, who nurtured and shaped it
And George,
who applauded loudest in his heart

What happens to a dream deferred?

Does it dry up
like a raisin in the sun?
Or fester like a sore —
And then run?
Does it stink like rotten meat?
Or crust and sugar over
like a syrupy sweet?

Maybe it just sags
like a heavy load.

Or does it explode?

—Langston Hughes

DAWN

Brewster Place was the bastard child of several clandestine meetings between the alderman of the sixth district and the managing director of Unico Realty Company. The latter needed to remove the police chief of the sixth district because he was too honest to take bribes and so had persisted in harassing the gambling houses the director owned. In turn, the alderman wanted the realty company to build their new shopping center on his cousin's property in the northern section of town. They came together, propositioned, bargained, and slowly worked out the consummation of their respective desires. As an afterthought, they agreed to erect four double-housing units on some worthless land in the badly crowded district. This would help to abate the expected protests from the Irish community over the police chief's dismissal; and since the city would underwrite the costs, and the alderman could use the construction to support his bid for mayor in the next election, it would importune neither man. And so in a damp, smoke-filled room, Brewster Place was conceived.

It was born three months later in the city legislature, and since its true parentage was hidden, half the community turned out for its baptism two years later. They applauded wildly as the smiling alderman smashed a bottle of champagne against the edge of one of the buildings. He could hardly be heard over the deafening cheers as he told them, with a tear in the corner of his eye, it was the least he could do to help make space for all their patriotic boys who were on the way home from the Great War.

The gray bricks of the buildings were the color of dull silver during Brewster Place's youth. Although the street wasn't paved—after a heavy rain it was necessary to wade in ankle-deep to get home—there was a sense of promise in the street and in the times. The city was growing and prospering; there were plans for a new boulevard just north of the street, and it seemed as if Brewster Place was to become part of the main artery of the town.

The boulevard became a major business district, but in order to control traffic some of the auxiliary streets had to be walled off. There was a fierce battle in the city legislature between the representatives of these small veins because they knew they were fighting for the lifeblood of their community, but there was no one to fight for Brewster Place. The neighborhood was now filled with people who had no political influence; people who were dark haired and mellow-skinned—Mediterraneans—who spoke to each other in rounded guttural sounds and who brought strange foods to the neighborhood stores. The older residents were offended by the pungent smells of strong cheeses and smoked meats that now hung in the local shops. So the wall came up and Brewster Place became a dead-end street. There were no crowds at this baptism, which took place at three o'clock in the morning when Mrs. Colligan's son, stumbling home drunk and forgetting the wall was there, bloodied his nose and then leaned over and vomited against the new bricks.

Brewster Place had less to offer the second generation of children—those of its middle years—but it did what it could for them. The street was finally paved under the WPA program, and a new realty company picked up the mortgage on the buildings. Cut off from the central activities of the city, the street developed a personality of its own. The people had their own language and music and codes. They prided themselves on the fact that Mrs. Fuelli's store was the only one in the city that carried scungilli and spinach fettucine. But it broke Mrs. Fuelli's heart when her son returned from the war and didn't settle on Brewster Place, and her cousin's son didn't either, or her second-floor neighbor's. And there were the sons who never returned at all. Brewster Place mourned with these mothers because it had lost children also—to the call of a more comfortable life and to the fear of these present children who were once strange but were now all it had. Brewster Place grew old with Mrs. Fuelli and the few others who either refused or were unable to leave.

A year before the Supreme Court decision in Brown v. Topeka Board of Education realigned the entire country, integration came to Brewster Place on the rounded shoulders of a short, brown-skinned man who had been hired as janitor and handyman for the buildings. He moved into the basement of 312, and when asked his name would reply, "Just call me Ben." And that's all he was to be known by until his death. There was little protest over his living in the block because it got around that he was a nice colored man who never bothered anybody. And when the landlord was a post-office box in another city, and the radiators leaked, or the sink backed up, or arthritis kept you from sweeping the front steps, it was convenient to have someone around to take care of those things, even this man with strange hair and skin and hints of stale liquor on his breath.

Ben and Brewster Place's Mediterraneans grew well acquainted from a distance. They learned that when they were awakened by the somber tones of "Swing Low, Sweet Chariot" he was on one of his early drunks, and there was no point in asking him to do anything that day—he would yessem you to distraction and just never show up. And he learned that no matter how great the quantities of homemade vegetable soup and honey nut loaves brought up to him by old ladies clucking softly about his womanless plight, he would be met with cold and suspicious eyes if he knocked on their doors without a wrench or broom in his hands. Conse-

*quently, no one ever knew why Ben drank. The more obser-
vant could predict the return of the early drunks because
they always occurred the morning after the mailman descended the basement steps of 312. And if anyone ventured
close enough the next day, Ben could be heard mumbling
about an unfaithful wife and a lame daughter, or was it a
lame wife and an unfaithful daughter? They could never tell
which. And if they cared to ask, he probably could have told
them, but after a while the mailman stopped descending those
steps; yet Ben still drank.*

*Ben and his drinking became a fixture on Brewster Place,
just like the wall. It soon appeared foolish to question the
existence of either—they just were. And they were the first
sight encountered by Brewster Place's third generation of
children, who drifted into the block and precipitated the ex-
odus of the remaining Mediterraneans. Brewster Place re-
joiced in these multi-colored "Afric" children of its old age.
They worked as hard as the children of its youth, and were
as passionate and different in their smells, foods, and codes
from the rest of the town as the children of its middle years.
They clung to the street with a desperate acceptance that
whatever was here was better than the starving southern cli-
mates they had fled from. Brewster Place knew that unlike
its other children, the few who would leave forever were to be
the exception rather than the rule, since they came because
they had no choice and would remain for the same reason.*

*Brewster Place became especially fond of its colored
daughters as they milled like determined spirits among its
decay, trying to make it a home. Nutmeg arms leaned over
windowsills, gnarled ebony legs carried groceries up double
flights of steps, and saffron hands strung out wet laundry on
back-yard lines. Their perspiration mingled with the steam
from boiling pots of smoked pork and greens, and it curled on
the edges of the aroma of vinegar douches and Evening in
Paris cologne that drifted through the street where they stood
together—hands on hips, straight-backed, round-bellied,
high-behinded women who threw their heads back when they*

laughed and exposed strong teeth and dark gums. They cursed, badgered, worshiped, and shared their men. Their love drove them to fling dishcloths in someone else's kitchen to help him make the rent, or to fling hot lye to help him forget that bitch behind the counter at the five-and-dime. They were hard-edged, soft-centered, brutally demanding, and easily pleased, these women of Brewster Place. They came, they went, grew up, and grew old beyond their years. Like an ebony phoenix, each in her own time and with her own season had a story.

MATTIE
MICHAEL

I

The rattling moving van crept up Brewster like a huge green slug. It was flanked by a battered gypsy cab that also drove respectfully over the hidden patches of ice under the day-old snow. It began to snow again, just as the small caravan reached the last building on the block.

The moving men jumped out of the front of the van and began to unload the back. Mattie paid the driver and got out of the cab. The moist gray air was as heavy as the sigh that lay on her full bosom. The ashen buildings were beginning to fade against the gentle blanketing of the furry gray snow coming from the darkening sky. The sun's dying rays could be felt rather than seen behind the leaden evening sky, and snow began to cling to the cracks in the wall that stood only six feet from her building.

Mattie saw that the wall reached just above the second-floor apartments, which meant the northern light would be blocked from her plants. All the beautiful plants that once had an entire sun porch for themselves in the home she had exchanged thirty years of her life to pay for would now have to fight for light on a crowded windowsill. The sigh turned into a knot of pity for the ones that she knew would die. She pitied them because she refused to pity herself and to think that she, too, would have to die here on this crowded street because there just wasn't enough life left for her to do it all again.

Someone was cooking on the first floor, and the aroma seeped through the misted window and passed across her nose. For a moment it smelled like freshly cut sugar cane, and she took in short, rapid breaths of air to try to capture the scent again. But it was gone. And it couldn't have been anyway. There was no sugar cane on Brewster. No, that had been in Tennessee, in a summer that lay under the graves of thirty-one years that could only be opened again in the mind.

Sugar cane and summer and Papa and Basil and Butch. And the beginning—the beginning of her long, winding journey to Brewster.

"Hey, gal."

A cinnamon-red man leaned over the Michaels' front fence and clucked softly to Mattie, who was in the yard feeding the young biddies. She purposely ignored him and ran her fingers around the pan to stir the mash and continued calling the chickens. He timed the clucking of his tongue with hers and called again, a little louder. "I say, hey, gal."

"I heard you the first time, Butch Fuller, but I got a name, you know," she said, without looking in his direction.

His long, upturned mouth, which always seemed ready to break into a smile, spread into a large grin, and he raced to the other edge of the fence and gave a deep exaggerated bow in front of her.

"Well, 'cuse us poor, ignorant niggers, Miz Mattie, mam, or shoulds I say, Miz Michael, mam, or shoulds I say Miz Mattie Michael, or shoulds I say Miz Mam, mam, or shoulds I . . ." And he threw her a look over his bowed shoulders that was a perfect imitation of the mock humility that they used on white people.

Mattie burst out laughing and Butch straightened up and laughed with her.

"Butch Fuller, you was born a fool and you'll die a fool."

"Well, least that'll give the preacher one good thing to say

8

at my funeral—this here man was consistent."

And they laughed again—Butch heartily and Mattie reluctantly—because she realized that she was being drawn into a conversation with a man her father had repeatedly warned her against. That Butch Fuller is a no-'count ditch hound, and no decent woman would be seen talkin' to him. But Butch had a laugh like the edges of an April sunset—translucent and mystifying. You knew it couldn't last forever, but you'd stand for hours, hoping for the chance to experience just a glimmer of it once again.

"Now that I done gone through all that, I hope I can get what I came for," he said slowly, as he looked her straight in the eyes.

The blood rushed to Mattie's face, and just as her mouth dropped open to fling an insult at him, he slid his eyes evenly over to the barrel at the side of the house. "A cup of that cool rain water." And he smiled wickedly.

She snapped her mouth shut, and he looked down and kicked the dust off his shoes, pretending not to notice her embarrassment.

"Yup, a scorcher like today is enough to make a man's throat just curl up and die." And he looked up innocently.

Mattie threw her feed pan down and walked sulkily to the rain barrel. Butch intently watched the circular movements of her high round behind under the thin summer dress, and he followed her rising hemline over the large dark calves when she bent to dip the water. But when she turned around, he was closely inspecting a snap on his overalls.

"Here's your water." She almost threw it at him. "I couldn't even deny a dog a drink on a day like today, but when you done drunk it, you better be gettin' on to wherever you was gettin' before you stopped."

"Lord, you Michael women got the sharpest tongues in the county, but I guess a man could die in a lot worst ways than being cut to death by such a beautiful mouth." And he threw his head back and drank the water.

Mattie watched the movement of the water as it passed

down his long throat, and she reluctantly admired the strong brown contours in his neck and arms. His skin looked as if it had sparks of fire in it, and the sun played against the red highlights in his body. He had clean, good-natured lines in his movements which seemed to say to everyone—I'm here and ain't complaining about it, so why are you?

"Thank you, Miz Mattie, mam." He handed the cup back to her with a special smile that beckoned friendship on the basis of the secret joke they now shared between them.

Mattie understood, took the cup, and returned his smile.

"And since you inquired on my wheretos and where-abouts . . ."

"I did no such thing."

He continued as if she hadn't spoken, "I'm on my way to the low ground to pick me some wild herbs. And then I plans to stop by the Morgans' sugar cane field near the levee. They just made harvest, and there's some nice fat canes left around. So if you care to come along and pick you out a few, I'd be more than obliged to carry 'em back this way for you."

Mattie almost agreed. She loved cane molasses, and if she found some really good ones, she could cut them up and boil them down and probably clear at least a pint or two of mo-lasses. But her father would kill her if he heard she had been seen walking with Butch Fuller.

"Of course, now, if a big woman like you is afraid of what her daddy might say?"

Mattie grew defiant, realizing that he had been reading her thoughts.

"I ain't afraid of nothing, Butch Fuller. And besides, Papa took Mama to town this afternoon."

"Why, well, just as I was saying . . . A big woman like you ain't got no cause to be scared of what her daddy might say. And as for them foul-minded old crows up on the hill who might run back to him with a pack of lies—why don't we just take the back road to the cane field? No point in letting them get sunstroke runnin' down the hill to tell something that really ain't nothin' to tell to somebody who ain't even here—right?" His voice was as smooth and coaxing as his smile.

"Right," she said, and then looking straight into his eyes added slowly, "now, just let me go into the house and get Papa's machete." She waited for the flicker of surprise to widen his eyes slightly and then continued, "To cut the cane with—of course."

"Of course." And the April sun set in its full glory.

The back road to the levee was winding and dusty. And August in Rock Vale was a time of piercing, dry heat—"sneaky heat," as the people called it. The moisture-free air felt almost comfortable, but then slowly the perspiration would begin to crawl down your armpits and plaster the clothes to your back. And the hot air in your lungs would expand until you felt that they were going to burst, so to relieve them you panted through a slightly opened mouth.

Mattie didn't think about the heat as she walked beside Butch. They were almost perfect company because he loved to talk and she was an intelligent listener, knowing intuitively when to interrupt with her own observations about some person or place. He amused her with slightly laundered tales of the happenings in the town's juke joints—places that were as foreign to her as Istanbul or Paris. And he scandalized her with his firsthand knowledge of who was seeing whose spouse down by the railroad tracks, just hours before they showed up at her church Sunday morning. He told her this gossip without judging or sneering, but with the same good-natured acceptance that he held toward everything in life. And Mattie found herself being shown how to laugh at things that would have been considered too shamefully ugly even to mention aloud at home.

She was so engrossed with Butch that she didn't see the approaching team of mules and wagon until it was almost upon them.

"Oh, no, it's Mr. Mike, the deacon of our church," she whispered to Butch, and stepped a full foot away from him and began to swing the machete as she walked.

The wagon and mules pulled up to them. "How do, Mattie. How do, Butch." And the old man spit a jawful of tobacco juice over the side of the wagon.

"Hey, Mr. Mike," Butch called out.

"Going to cut cane, Mr. Mike," Mattie chimed up loudly, and give the machete an extra swing to underscore her words.

Mr. Mike grinned. "Ain't figure you to be goin' catfishing with that knife, gal. Ain't you all taking the long way to the levee, though?" He sat watching them, chewing slowly on his tobacco.

Mattie could think of nothing to say and swung the machete as if the answer lay in the widening arc of the blade.

"Too much sun on the main road," Butch said easily. "And since black means poor in these parts—Lord knows, I couldn't stand to get no poorer."

Butch and Mr. Mike laughed, and Mattie tried not to look as miserable as she felt.

"Gal, stop swingin' that knife 'fore you chop off a leg," Mr. Mike said. "You plan on boiling up some cane molasses?"

"Yes, sir, Mr. Mike."

"Good then, if you get enough, bring me a taste Sunday. I love fresh cane syrup with my biscuits."

"Sure will, Mr. Mike."

He hit the reins and the mules started moving. "'Member me to your ma and daddy."

"Yes, sir."

"See you in church Sunday, Mattie." He called over his shoulder, "See you there doomsday, Butch."

"Or somewhere thereabouts, Mr. Mike."

The old man chuckled and spit over the side of the wagon again.

Mattie and Butch walked in silence for the next five minutes. He still had that crooked smile on his face, but there was something about the stiffness of his gait that told her that he was angry. He seemed to have closed off his spirit from her.

"My, Butch, you sure can think fast," she complimented,

in way of reconciliation. "I just didn't know what excuse to give him."

"Why give any!" The words exploded from his mouth. " 'Going to cut cane, Mr. Mike,' " he mimicked in a falsetto. "Whyn't you just haul up your dress and show him that your drawers was still glued to your legs? That's what you meant, wasn't it?"

"Now, why you gotta go and get nasty? Ain't nobody thinkin' 'bout that."

"Quit lying, Mattie. Don't you think I know what them sanctimonious folks like your daddy say about me?"

Mattie rose to her father's defense. "Well, you do got a bad reputation."

"Why? 'Cause I live my life and 'low other folks to live theirs? 'Cause if I had a pretty black gal like you for a daughter, I wouldn't have her nigh on twenty-one years old and not keeping company so she's so dumb she don't know her ass from her elbow? What he savin' you up for—his self?"

Mattie stopped abruptly. "Papa was right after all. You is nothin' but a filthy, low-down ditch dog! And I musta been crazy to think I could spend a civil afternoon with you." And she turned back toward home.

Butch grabbed her arm. "Lord have mercy, I must be improving in his sight! He forgot to add no-'count. You think that's sufficient encouragement for me to come callin' Sunday evening?" He said this with a mock innocence that was masterly devoid of any sarcasm.

In spite of herself, Mattie had to bite on her bottom lip to hold back a smile. "For your information, Mr. Fuller, I already keep company on Sunday afternoons."

"With who?"

"Fred Watson."

"Gal, that ain't keeping company. That's sitting up at a wake."

The stifled smile broke through her compressed lips as she thought of those boring evenings with the deadpan Fred Watson, but he was the only man in the church that her father thought good enough for her.

"And here I was all set to get jealous or something, and you come talkin' about old dead Fred. Why, I could come in there and steal you away with two full suitcases 'fore Fred would be able to blink an eye. You notice it takes him twice as long to blink than most folks?"

"I ain't noticed no such thing," Mattie lied.

Butch looked at her out of the corner of his eye. "Well, the next time you and Fred are sittin' on your daddy's front porch in one of them hot, passionate courtin' sessions—'fore you nod off to sleep—notice how he blinks."

I will not laugh, Mattie kept repeating to herself; I will not laugh even if I have to burst open and die.

They soon came to the edge of the cane field, and Butch took the machete from her and went through the tall grass, picking out the best stalks. She felt disquieting stirrings at the base of her stomach and in her fingertips as she watched his strong lean body bend and swing the wide-bladed knife against the green and brownish stalks.

Whenever he came upon one that was especially ripe, he would hold it over his head, his two muscled arms glistening with sweat, and call out, "This one's like you, Mattie—plump and sweet," or, "Lord, see how that beautiful gal is makin' me work."

She knew it was all in fun. Everything about Butch was like puffed air and cotton candy, but it thrilled her anyway whenever he straightened up to call to her through the tall grass.

When he had cut about a dozen canes, he gathered them up and brought them out to the edge of the field. He kneeled down, took some cord from his pocket, and bound the stalks into two bundles. When he got off his knees, he smelled like a mixture of clean sweat, raw syrup, and topsoil. He took a bundle of cane under each arm.

"Mattie, reach into my overall top and pull my kerchief. This sweat is blindin' me."

She was conscious of the hardness of his chest under her

probing fingers as she sought the handkerchief, and when she stood on her toes to wipe his wet brow, her nipples brushed the coarse denim of his overalls and began to strain against the thin dress. These new feelings confused Mattie, and she felt that she had somehow drifted too far into strange waters and if she didn't turn around soon, she would completely forget in which direction the shore lay—or worse, not even care.

"Well, we got our cane. Let's get home," she said abruptly.

"Now, ain't that just like a woman?" Butch shifted the heavy stalks. "Bring a man clear out of his way to cut three times as much cane as he needed for hisself and then want to double-time him back home before he gets a minute's rest or them wild herbs he really came all this way fo'."

"Aw right." Mattie sucked her teeth impatiently and picked up the machete. "Where's the herb patch?"

"Just by the clearing of them woods."

The temperature dropped at least ten degrees on the edge of the thick, tangled dogwood, and the deep green basil and wild thyme formed a fragrant blanket on the mossy earth. Butch dropped the cane and sank down on the ground with a sigh.

"Jesus, this is nice," he said, looking around and inhaling the cool air. He seemed puzzled that Mattie was still standing. "Lord, gal, ain't your feet tired after all that walking?"

Mattie cautiously sat down on the ground and put her father's machete between them. The refreshing dampness of the forest air did little to relieve the prickling heat beneath her skin.

"You blaspheme too much," she said irritably. "You ain't supposed to use the Lord's name in vain."

Butch shook his head. "You folks and your ain'ts. You ain't supposed to do this and you ain't supposed to do that. That's why I never been no Christian—to me it means you can't enjoy life and since we only here once, that seems a shame."

"Nobody said nothin' about not enjoying life, but I suppose runnin' after every woman that moves is your idea of enjoyment?" Mattie was trying desperately to work up a righteous anger against Butch. She needed something to neutralize the lingering effect of his touch and smell.

"Mattie, I don't run after a lot of women, I just don't stay long enough to let the good times turn sour. Ya know, befo' the two of us get into a rut and we're cussing and fighting and just holding on because we done forgot how to let go. Ya see, all the women I've known can never remember no bad days with me. So when they stuck with them men who are ignorin' 'em or beatin' and cheatin' on 'em, they sit up on their back porches shelling peas and they thinks about old Butch, and they say, Yeah, that was one sweet, red nigger—all our days were sunlight; maybe it was a short time, but it sure felt good."

What he said made sense to Mattie, but there was something remiss in his reasoning and she couldn't quite figure out what it was.

"Now you think about it," he said, "how many women I ever went with ever had anything ornery to say about me? Maybe their mamas or papas had something to say," and he smiled slyly across the grass, "or their husbands—but never them. Think about it."

She searched her mind and, surprisingly, couldn't come up with one name.

Butch grinned triumphantly as he watched her face and could almost see the mental checklist she was running through.

"Well," Mattie threw at him, "there's probably a couple I just ain't met."

Butch laid his head back and his laughter lit up the dark trees.

"Lord, that's what I like about you Michael women—you hardly ever at a loss for words. Mattie, Mattie Michael," he chanted softly under his breath, his eyes caressing her face. "Where'd you get a sir name like Michael? Shouldn't it be Michaels?"

"Naw, Papa said that when the emancipation came, his daddy was just a little boy, and he had been hard of hearing so his master and everyone on the plantation had to call him twice to get his attention. So his name being Michael, they always called him Michael-Michael. And when the Union census taker came and was registering black folks, they asked what my granddaddy's name was, and they said Michael-Michael was all they knew. So the dumb Yankee put that down and we been Michael ever since."

Mattie's father loved telling her that story, and she in turn enjoyed repeating it to anyone who questioned her strange last name. As she talked, Butch was careful not to let his eyes wander below her neck. He knew she was sitting over there like a timid starling, poised for flight. And the slightest movement on his part would frighten her away for good.

So he listened to her with his eyes intently on her face while his mind slipped down the ebony neck that was just plump enough for a man to bury his nose into and suck up tiny bits of flesh that were almost as smooth as the skin on the top of her full round breasts that held nipples that were high, tilted, and unbelievably even darker than the breasts, so that when they touched the tongue there was the sensation of drinking rich, double cocoa. A man could spend half a lifetime there alone, but the soft mound of her belly whispered to him, and his mind reached down and kneaded it ever so gently until it was supple and waiting. And then the tip of his tongue played round and round the small cavern in the center of her stomach, while the hands tried to memorize every curve and texture of the inner thighs and lightly pressed outward to widen the legs so they could move through them and get lost in the eternity of softness on her behind. And she would wait and wait, getting fuller and fuller until finally pleading with him to do something—anything—to stop the expansion before she burst open her skin and lay in a million pieces among the roots of the trees and the leaves of the tiny basil.

When Mattie finished her story, Butch was looking down at the sugar cane and tracing the handle of his jackknife along the thick segmented ridges.

"You know how to eat sugar cane, Mattie?" he asked, still tracing the ridges. He avoided looking at her, afraid of what she would read in his eyes.

"You a crazy nigger, Butch Fuller. First you ask me 'bout my name and then come up with some out-the-way question like that. I been eating sugar cane all my life, fool!"

"Naw," Butch said, "some folks die and never learn how to eat cane the right way." He got on his knees, broke off one of the stalks, and began to peel it with his knife. He was speaking so softly Mattie had to lean closer to hear him.

"You see," he said, "eating cane is like living life. You gotta know when to stop chewing—when to stop trying to wrench every last bit of sweetness out of a wedge—or you find yourself with a jawful of coarse straw that irritates your gums and the roof of your mouth."

The thick blade of the knife slid under the heavy green covering on the stalk, and clear, beady juices sprang to the edges and glistened in the dying afternoon sun.

"The trick," he said, cutting off a slice of the stiff, yellow fiber, "is to spit it out while the wedge is still firm and that last bit of juice—the one that promises to be the sweetest of the whole mouthful—just escapes the tongue. It's hard, but you gotta spit it out right then, or you gonna find yourself chewing on nothin' but straw in that last round. Ya know what I mean, Mattie?"

He finally looked her straight in the face, and Mattie found herself floating far away in the brown sea of his irises, where the words, shoreline and anchor, became like gibberish in some foreign tongue.

"Here," he said, holding out a piece of the cane wedge to her, "try it the way I told you."

And she did.

II

Mattie's father had not spoken a word to either her or his wife in two days. The torturing silence in the house was far worse than the storm that Mattie had prepared herself to take when her mother had told him about her pregnancy. Samuel Michael had never been a talkative man, but his calm, steady habits had brought a sense of security and consistency to their home. Mattie had been the only child of his autumn years, and so for as long as she could remember, he had been an old man with set and exacting ways. Unlike her mother he never raised his voice, and when the two had a difference of opinion, her mother would charge around the house, mumbling and banging pans, while he would just sit on the porch rocker and read his Bible.

Once Mattie had wanted a pair of patent-leather pumps like the girls in town, and her mother had said they were too expensive and impractical for their dusty country roads. Sam refused to take sides in the battle over the shoes, which lasted for weeks, but he went and hired himself out in the sweet potato fields for a month of Saturdays, brought home the shoes, and dropped them in her lap—wear 'em only on Sundays were his first and last words on the matter.

His had been the first face Mattie had seen when she opened her eyes after a week of blinding scarlet fever. He had simply touched her forehead and went to call her mother to come and change her nightgown. It was her mother, and not him, who later told her that he had neglected his farm and insisted on sitting by her bed every day—all day—while the life was burning and sweating out of her pores. It became a legend in those parts, and even her mother never knew how he had gotten the white doctor from town to make that long trip to the house for her. Sam never mentioned it, and no one dared ask.

But this silence was different. It was compressed tightly

in a vacuum that was so vast that her spirit grew weary attempting to cross it, and so it would return to her to rest feverishly against her sorrowing heart.

"Mama, I can't stand much more of this," she whispered miserably to her mother, as they were washing the dinner dishes.

Her father had stonily finished his meal and gone out to his rocker, where he would sit reading his Bible until late in the night.

"Don't worry, baby," Fannie sighed, "he'll come round. This here thing done hurt him, that's all."

"Oh, Mama, I'm so ashamed."

"Ain't nothing to be shamed of. Havin' a baby is the most natural thing there is. The Good Book call children a gift from the Lord. And there ain't no place in that Bible of His that say babies is sinful. The sin is the fornicatin', and that's over and done with. God done forgave you of that a long time ago, and what's going on in your belly now ain't nothin' to hang your head about—you remember that."

"You didn't tell him it was Butch, did you?"

"Gal, you think I want to see my man in jail for killin' the likes of Butch Fuller? And besides, it ain't for me to tell."

They heard the screen door slam shut.

"Butt, come here," Sam called.

Mattie jumped at the unaccustomed sound of his voice. She was finally being summoned across that vacuum, and her spirit rose instinctively to obey, but she held it back in fear of what it might meet there. She looked pleadingly at her mother for help in this dilemma, and the older woman patted her shoulder and whispered in her ear, "Go on now. I told you he'd come round. That man lives and breathes for you."

She looked out the kitchen door and couldn't find the courage to move toward the stiff-backed old man, who was staring into the empty fireplace with a face as still and unreadable as a worn stone. So she moved toward the dying vibrations of the nickname, Butt. And it was the memory of the man who used to roll her full cheeks between his fingers and chuckle—soft as a dish of butter—that got her across the room.

"Yes, Papa," she trembled.

Mattie knew to keep silent and wait. There would be nothing she could explain or plead or reason at that moment that would change the direction that his mind had locked into, like rusted iron clogs.

"I been thinkin' on this here thing," he began quietly, without looking around. There was a long pause. "I done always tried to do my best by you. I seen that you never had a hungry day or had to go askin' nobody for nothin', ain't it?"

"Yes, Papa."

He cleared his throat and continued slowly, "I know some say I put too much store in you, keepin' you too close to home, settin' you up to be better'n other folks. But I done what I saw fit at the time to do."

Mattie gradually began to realize what he had been struggling with the past two days. He couldn't bring himself to accept any fault within her, and since he needed someone to do retribution, he had laid the blame for this on his own shoulders. She saw with pity how stooped and faltering the proud man was carrying this burden. She rushed in vain to relieve him of it.

"Papa, you ain't done nothing wrong. This—"

He cut her off. "Could be, I should have let you marry that Harris boy you was sweet on once, but I wanted better for you than some wanderin' field hand and him wanting to drag you all the way to Arkansas, away from your family and all. Well, past is past. And I still think Fred Watson is a tolerable young man, in spite of what he done." He cleared his throat again and looked up at her. "I was young once, too. And done made many a mistake and ain't through makin' 'em."

Mattie was stunned that he would think it was Fred's baby. But then, that was the only man he had allowed her to see, and his mind had been so conditioned over the years to her unquestioning obedience that there was just no space for doubt. She listened with horror as he continued.

"So I figure to go over to his place tomorrow after breakfast and clear this all up. I know he'll be willing to do right by you."

Mattie wanted to choke. She felt as if the entire universe had been formed into a ball and jammed into her throat—"Papa, it ain't Fred's baby"—sent it hurling out of her mouth and into a whirlwind that crumbled her father's face and exploded both of their hearts into uncountable pieces. She saw them both being spun around the room and sucked out of the windows along with everything that had ever passed between them. She felt the baby being drawn by the winds, but she held on tightly, trembling violently, because she realized that now this was all she would ever have.

"Whose is it?" came to her over the dying winds of the tempest, but her ears were still ringing and she couldn't quite make out the sounds.

"I say, whose is it?" And he came toward her, grabbed her by the back of the hair, and yanked her face upward to confront the blanket of rage in his eyes.

Instinctively her body cried out to obey—to tell him that it was Butch's so he would release her and grab his shotgun and go out and blow Butch into as many pieces as her world now lay in around her. She didn't care about Butch Fuller, and they had hardly spoken since that day, but this baby didn't really belong to him. It belonged to something out there in the heat of an August day and the smell of sugar cane and mossy herbs. Mattie knew there were no words for this, and even if there were, this disappointed and furious old man would never understand.

"I ain't saying, Papa." And she braced herself for the impact of the large calloused hand that was coming toward her face. He still held her by the hair so she took the force of the two blows with her neck muscles, and her eyes went dim as the blood dripped down her chin from her split lip. The grip on her hair tightened, and she was forced even closer to his face as she answered the silent question in his narrowing eyes.

"I ain't saying, Papa," she mumbled through her swollen lip.

"You'll say," he whispered hoarsely, as he yanked her to the ground by the hair.

She heard her mother rush from the kitchen. "That's enough, Sam."

"Stay out of this, Fannie." He picked up the broom that was leaning against the fireplace and held it threateningly in the air. "Now, you tell me or I'll beat it out of you."

Her silence stole the last sanctuary for his rage. He wanted to kill the man who had sneaked into his home and distorted the faith and trust he had in his child. But she had chosen this man's side against him, and in his fury, he tried to stamp out what had hurt him the most and was now brazenly taunting him—her disobedience.

Mattie's body contracted in a painful spasm each time the stick smashed down on her legs and back, and she curled into a tight knot, trying to protect her stomach. He would repeat his question with each blow from the stick, and her continued silence caused the blows to come faster and harder. He was sweating and breathing so hard he couldn't talk anymore, so he just pounded the whimpering girl on the floor.

Her mother screamed, "For the love of Jesus, Sam!" and jumped on his back and tried to wrestle the stick from him.

He flung her across the floor and her blouse tore to the waist as she went sliding into the opposite wall.

"Oh, God, oh, God," Fannie chanted feverishly, as she got up on her bruised knees.

The broom had broken, and he was now kneeling over Mattie and beating her with a jagged section of it that he had in his fist.

"Oh, God, oh, God," Fannie kept saying, as she searched blindly around the room. She finally found the shotgun pegged over the front door. She struggled with the heavy gun, and her hand was trembling so much it was difficult to load the bulky shells, but she got them in and snapped the gun shut. She wrapped her finger around the trigger, aimed, and pulled. The force of the gun's blast almost knocked her off her feet. The edge of the fireplace exploded and sent flying bits of bricks into Mattie's back and cut up the right side of her father's face.

The blast stunned him for a moment, and he looked toward his wife with sweat and blood dripping down his face.

"So help me Jesus, Sam!" she screamed. "Hit my child again, and I'll meet your soul in hell!"

She cocked the gun again and this time aimed for the center of his chest.

"Look! Just look a' what you done!"

Sam seemed like a man coming out of a trance. He stared stupidly at the barrel of the gun and then at the stick in his fist and then at the girl balled up in spasms on the floor. His head kept moving numbly back and forth, like a badly timed mechanical toy.

"Fannie, I . . . Fannie, she . . ." he mumbled dazedly.

A slow moan came from the pile of torn clothes and bruised flesh on the floor. Sam Michael looked at it, saw that it was his daughter, and he dropped the stick and wept.

III

A week later the northbound Greyhound pulled across the county line, turned right on the Interstate, and headed toward its first stop in Asheville, North Carolina. It was one of a legion of buses, trains, and rusting automobiles that carried the dark children of the South toward the seductive call of wartime jobs and freedom in urban areas above the Mason-Dixon. Mattie sat in an aisle seat and tried to ignore the melting of familiar landscapes. She didn't want to think about the strange city that lay ahead or even of her friend Etta, who would be at the depot to meet her. And she didn't want to think about the home that had been lost to her, or her mother's parting tears, or the painful breach with her father that throbbed as much as the soreness that was still in her back and legs. She just wanted to lay her head on the cushioned seat and suspend time, pretend that she had been born that very moment on that very bus, and that this was all there was and ever would be. But just then the baby moved, and she put her hands on her stomach and knew that she was nurturing within her what had gone before and would come after. This child would tie her to that past and future as inextricably as it was now tied to her every heartbeat.

So as Rock Vale, Tennessee, was buried under the miles of concrete that ribboned behind the bus, Mattie worried and planned for the child within her. When her mind would reach out behind, she forced herself to think only of the back road to the house, the feel of summer, the taste of sugar cane, and the smell of wild herbs. And when her son was born five months later, she named him Basil.

"Well, look a here," Etta marveled as she stroked the cracked red fist of the baby. "We come a long way from the time the old folks told us babies were mailed from heaven. 'C.O.D. or Special Delivery?' you'd ask, and set 'em all a howling. Guess you know what it's all about now?"

"Oh, no, Etta," Mattie looked up at her friend with her son mirrored in her eyes, "they still do. Isn't he the most perfect thing you ever saw?"

"Hardly that," Etta teased, as she took the baby from Mattie's lap. "He's ugly and wrinkled as a monkey, like most newborns. But I do see definite possibilities. Yup, I think we got the makings here of the first colored President."

Their laughter startled the baby, and he began to cry. "Lord, he's starting to squall! Here, take him. There, now, there's your mama."

She gave him back to Mattie and watched as she gently rocked and patted him to sleep. "See why I can't have no children? I ain't got the patience for all that."

"No one does, Etta, but it comes—when you know it's yours and you have to do for it. And you are mine, ain't you?" she whispered to the sleeping baby. "All mine."

"That's right, all yours—built-in heartache for the next twenty years. Now me, when I want ready-made trouble, I dig up a handsome man. No diapers to change, and I can walk when I'm ready. And that's just about what I'm fixin' to do; Bennett is starting to fray my nerves."

Mattie looked up, stricken. "You leaving?"

"Yeah, honey. I was ready months ago, but when you wrote and said you were comin', I stuck around to see you settled with the baby. But this town is dead."

"Where to now, Etta?" she asked with a sigh.

"Honey, New York is the place to be! All those soldier boys are just pullin' up to the docks with pocketfuls of combat pay and lookin' for someone to help 'em invest it. And there's a place called Harlem with nothing but wall-to-wall colored doctors and real estate men. Why don't you come with me, Mattie? With all them possibilities, you bound to find Basil a rich daddy."

Etta's enthusiasm had almost convinced her, but then she caught herself. "Oh, no," Mattie shook her head, "I'm not dragging my baby all over the country behind you. When you first left home, you wrote and said St. Louis was the place to be, and then it was Chicago, and then here. Now it's New York. You ain't gonna find whatever it is you lookin' for that way."

"Well, I ain't gonna find it sittin' here, either. And neither will you."

"I ain't lookin' for nothing, Etta." She stared down at her son. "I got everything I need right here. And I'm content to stay put with what God gave me."

"Well," Etta said, going toward the door, "the way I heard it, God got out of the baby business after Jesus was born, but maybe you know something I don't." And she winked and left.

"What I know," Mattie said to the closed door, "is that this boy did come C.O.D., and I'm willin' to stay here and pay for it."

Etta left Mattie six weeks later with eight cases of condensed milk and coupon books for fifty pounds of sugar. Mattie didn't dare ask where they had come from because she knew Etta would tell her. In the loneliness that rushed in to fill the vacuum her friend had left, she found herself thinking of home, and she longed to see her mother. She wrote and asked her to come stay with the baby while she went to work because she didn't want to leave him with strangers. Her mother wrote back that she wanted to come, but her father was doing poorly and she couldn't leave him, but, please, send the baby down there while she worked.

Mattie looked around at the cramped boardinghouse room with its cheap furniture and dingy walls that no amount of scrubbing seemed to lighten, and she thought of the organdy curtains and the large front yard in her parents' home—the clean air and fresh food. But each day her baby was beginning to look unmistakably like Butch, and she thought of the unbending old man who would sit with his Bible clenched in his fist and watch him grow up.

"I can't put you through that," she whispered. "Right now I can't give you much, but you're too little to see this room anyway. All you see is your mama, right? And you know Mama loves you and accepts you—no matter how you got here."

As if in answer Basil began to kick his arms and legs and whine. Mattie picked him up and pressed his soft body to her bosom, molding him into her heart as he went to sleep.

She found an assembly-line job in a book bindery, and she paid Mrs. Prell, an old woman on the first floor, to keep him during the day. Mattie thought the woman appeared a bit senile, and she had three cats. To save carfare, Mattie would walk the thirty blocks back to the boardinghouse to see the baby during her lunch break. She had just enough time to rush in, pick him up, see if he was wet or marked in some way, and then go back to work. She resorted to eating her lunch while she rushed through the streets, because she got dizzy in the afternoon from the heat of the factory and the smell of the strong glue on an empty stomach.

Mattie couldn't seem to save enough money to move. The babysitter cost her almost half of her weekly salary, and after she paid a week's rent and bought some food, there was just enough left over for carfare. She stopped going to the movies on Saturday nights and only bought clothes or shoes when hers had reached the state where she was ashamed of being seen in the streets. Yet her bank account grew painfully slowly. And then Basil developed a stomach condition and couldn't keep his food down. So her small reserve went for a specialist and expensive medicine.

She thought about taking night courses at school in order to get a better job, but what with working six days a week, she hardly ever saw the baby as it was. It was heartbreaking when she missed his first step, and she had cried for two hours when she first heard him call Mrs. Prell "Mama."

One Friday night Mattie was asleep with Basil, and he had squirmed out of her arms and lay on his stomach near the edge of the bed. His bottle had fallen out of his mouth and rolled on the floor next to the blanket. A rat crept out of the hole behind the dresser and cautiously sniffed around the wall for crumbs. Finding nothing, it grew bolder in its search and circled slowly toward the bed. It had learned to fear the human smell but the stillness of the bodies and its hunger drew it nearer to the bed. It was about to turn away and begin a new search toward the wall when it smelled the dried milk and sugar. Giving a squeak of anticipation, it edged toward the smell and found the baby's bottle. It licked the sweet crusted milk around the hole of the nipple and tried to gnaw through the thick rubber. Then the same smell drifted down from above its head, and, abandoning the nipple, it crawled up the blanket toward the fresh aroma of milk, sugar, and saliva. It licked around the baby's chin and lips, and when there was nothing left, it sought more and sank its fangs into the soft flesh.

Basil's screams sent Mattie bolt upright in the bed, and in her sleepy confusion she instinctively hugged her arms to her and found them empty. She felt something leap from the bed and scramble across the wooden floor toward the dresser. She reached out blindly for the howling child, grabbed him to her chest, and stumbled toward the light switch. The sudden movements and brightness of the room frightened the child even more, and he kicked and fought her in his confusion and pain.

"Oh, God!" she cried as she saw the blood dripping down his cheek from the two small punctures. She tried to calm the wailing child against her chest but he sensed her fear and continued to scream. She put him on the bed and cleaned his cheek with alcohol and rocked and soothed him down into a whimper. She reached for his bottle and, seeing the gnawed nipple, threw it against the wall in anger and disgust. The shattering glass frightened the child again, and he began to cry and Mattie cried with him.

She sat up all night with the lights on, and Basil finally fell into a fitful sleep. The next morning she took him to the hospital for a tetanus shot and ointment for his cheek. She returned to the boardinghouse, picked up her clothes, and with her baby in one arm and her suitcase in the other, she went looking for another place to live.

"We don't take children."
"I'll pay anything."
"We don't take children!"

She walked the entire day, and her hand became blistered from the handle of the suitcase. Basil was growing heavy and restless in her arms, and his constant whining and struggling was taxing her strength. She had thought that she would find another place within hours, but her choices were few. After countless attempts, she learned that there was no need in wasting her energy to climb to steps in the white neighborhoods that displayed vacancy signs, and she even learned to shun certain neatly manicured black neighborhoods.

"Where's your husband?"
"I ain't got one."
"This is a respectable place!"

As the evening approached she cursed the aching feet that were beginning to fail her and she cursed her haste in leaving the only shelter they had, but then she thought about the gnawed bottle nipple and kept walking. She had her week's pay; she could go to a hotel. She could buy a one-way ticket home. Tomorrow was Sunday; she could look again. She could go home. If she found nothing Sunday, she could try again Monday. She could go home. If nothing Monday, she must show at work for Tuesday. Who would keep the baby? She could go home. Home. Home.

In her confusion Mattie had circled the same block twice. She remembered passing that old white woman just minutes before. She must have wandered into one of their neighborhoods again. She started to approach her and ask for directions to the bus station, but she changed her mind. She shifted Basil in her arms and silently walked past the fence.

"Where you headin' with that pretty red baby? You lost, child?"

Mattie looked for the direction of the voice.

"If you wants the bus depot, you walkin' in the wrong direction, 'cause nobody in their right mind would be trying to walk to the train station. It's clear on the other side of town."

Mattie realized that the old woman was actually talking to her, but it was a black voice. She hesitantly approached the fence and stared incredulously into a pair of watery blue eyes.

"What you gapin' at? You simple-minded or something? I asked if you lost?"

Mattie saw that the evening light had hidden the yellow undertones in the finely wrinkled white face, and it had softened the broad contours of the woman's pug nose and full lips.

"Yes, mam. I mean, no, mam," she stammered. "I was looking for a place to stay and couldn't find none, so I was looking for the bus depot, I guess," she finished confusedly.

"What, you plan on sleeping in the depot with that baby tonight?"

"No, I was gonna buy a ticket and go home, I guess, or find a hotel and try again tomorrow, or maybe find a place on the way to the depot. I don't know, I . . ." Mattie stopped talking because she knew she probably sounded like a complete fool to the woman, but she was so tired that she couldn't think, and her legs were starting to tremble from lack of sleep and the heavy load she had carried around all day. She bit on her bottom lip to hold back the tears that were burning the corner of her eyes.

"Well, where'd you sleep last night?" the woman said softly. "You get kicked out?"

"No, mam." And Mattie told her about the boardinghouse and the rat.

"And you just pick up and leave with no place to stay? Ain't that a caution. Whyn't you just plug up the hole with some steel wool and stay there till you could get better?"

Mattie tightened her arm around Basil and shook her head. There was no way she could have slept another night in that place without nightmares of things that would creep out of the walls to attack her child. She could never take him back to a place that had caused him so much pain.

The woman looked at the way she held the child and understood.

"Ya know, you can't keep him runnin' away from things that hurt him. Sometimes, you just gotta stay there and teach him how to go through the bad and good of whatever comes."

Mattie grew impatient with the woman. She didn't want a lecture about taking care of her son.

"If you'll just show me the way to the depot, I'll be obliged, mam," she said coldly. "Or if you know somewhere that has a room."

The woman chuckled. "No need to go gettin' snippy. That's one of the privileges of old age—you can give plenty of advice 'cause most folks think that's all you got left anyway. Now I may know of something available and I may not," she said, her eyes narrowing. "You workin'?"

Mattie told her where she worked.

"Where's your husband?"

Mattie knew this question was coming, and she was tempted to say that he had been killed in the war, but that would be a denial of her son, and she felt nothing shameful about what he was.

"I ain't got one." And she bent down and picked up her suitcase.

"Well," the old woman chuckled, "I've had five—outlived 'em all. So I can tell you, you ain't missing much." She opened the gate. "Since you done already picked up your valise, you might as well come on in and get that boy out the night air. Got plenty of room here. Just me and my grandbaby. He'll be good company for Lucielia."

She took Basil from Mattie's arms. "Lord, he's heavy. How'd you tote him all day? Look a' them fat legs, pretty red thing, you. I was always partial to reddish men. My second husband was his color, but did he have a temper." And she cooed and talked to the baby and Mattie as if she had known them for years.

Mattie followed her up the stone steps, trying to adjust her mind to this rapid turn of events and the nameless old woman who had altered their destinies. They entered the house and she set her suitcase on the thick green carpet and looked around the huge living room overcrowded with expensive mahogany furniture and china bric-a-brac. Through a door on the right, a yellowing crystal and brass chandelier hung over an oak table large enough to seat twelve people.

"Don't mind the house, child. I know it's a mess but I

ain't got the strength I once had to keep it tidy. I guess you all must be hungry. Come on in the kitchen." And she headed for the back of the house with the baby.

Mattie was beginning to collect herself. "But I don't even know your name!" she called out, still fixed to the living room floor.

The old woman turned around. "That mean you can't eat my food? Well, since you gotta be properly introduced, the name of what's in the kitchen is pot roast, oven-browned potatoes, and string beans. And I believe there's even some angel food cake waitin' to make your acquaintance." She started toward the kitchen again and threw over her shoulder, "And the crazy old woman you're sure by now you're talkin' to is Eva Turner."

Mattie hurried behind Eva and Basil into the kitchen.

"I meant no offense, Mrs. Turner. It's just that this was all so quick and you've really been kind and my name is Mattie Michael and this is Basil and I don't even know how much space you got for us or how much you want to charge or anything, so you can see why I'm a little confused, can't you?" she finished helplessly.

The woman listened to her rattled introduction with calm amusement. "People 'round here call me Miss Eva." She put the baby on the polished tile floor and went to the stove. She seemed to ignore Mattie and hummed to herself while she heated and stirred the food.

Mattie was beginning to wonder if the woman might actually be a bit insane, and she looked around the kitchen for some sign of it. All she saw was rows of polished copper pots, huge potted plants, and more china bric-a-brac. There was a child's playpen pushed in the corner with piles of colorful rubber toys. Basil had seen the toys also and was tottering toward them. Mattie went to stop him, and he cried out in protest.

Miss Eva turned from the stove. "Leave him be. He ain't botherin' nothing. Them's Lucielia's toys, and she's asleep now."

"Who's Lucielia?" Mattie asked.

Miss Eva looked as if she were now doubting Mattie's sanity. "I told you outside—that's my son's child. I've had her since she was six months old. Her parents went back to Tennessee and just left the baby. Neither of 'em are worth the spit it takes to cuss 'em. But then, I can't blame her daddy none. He takes after his father—my last husband, who I shouldn't of never married, but I was always partial to dark-skinned men."

She brought the plates of food to the table, and while Mattie ate, Miss Eva insisted on feeding Basil. Mattie didn't know if it was the seasoned food or the warm air in the kitchen, but she felt herself settling like fine dust on her surroundings and accepting the unexplained kindness of the woman with a hunger of which she had been unaware. In the unabashed fashion of the old, Miss Eva unfolded her own life and secret exploits to Mattie, and without realizing she was being questioned, Mattie found herself talking about things that she had buried within her. The young black woman and the old yellow woman sat in the kitchen for hours, blending their lives so that what lay behind one and ahead of the other became indistinguishable.

"Child, I know what you talkin' about. My daddy was just like that, too. I remember the night I ran off with my first husband, who was a singer. My daddy hunted us down for three months and then drug me home and kept me locked in my room for weeks with the windows all nailed up. But soon as he let me out, Virgil came back and got me, and we was off again." She laughed heartily at the memory. "We joined the vaudeville circuit and went on stage. My daddy didn't speak to me for years, but I couldn't stay away from that Virgil. I was always partial to brown-skinned men."

Mattie was puzzled. "But I thought you said before that you were partial to—"

"Ain't it a fact." Miss Eva's face spread into a wicked grin. "Well, if the truth be told, I likes 'em all, but they don't seem to agree with me—like fried onions. You like fried onions? I'll make us some liver and fried onions for Sunday supper tomorrow."

"That would be nice, mam, but you haven't told me yet what it'll cost to stay here with our room and board."

"I ain't runnin' no boardinghouse, girl; this is my home. But there's spare room upstairs that you're welcome to, along with the run of the house."

"But I can't stay without paying something," Mattie insisted, "and with you offering to mind the baby, too—I can't take advantage like that. Please, what will it cost?"

"All right," Miss Eva said, as she looked at the sleeping child in her arms, "I ain't decided yet, but in time I'll let you know."

Mattie was too sleepy to argue any further; she could hardly keep her eyes open. Miss Eva showed her to the bedroom upstairs, and Mattie was to die with the memory of the smell of lemon oil and the touch of cool, starched linen on her first night—of the thirty years of nights—she would spend in that house.

And she lay down with her son and sank into a timeless sleep. Time's passage through the memory is like molten glass that can be opaque or crystallize at any given moment at will: a thousand days are melted into one conversation, one glance, one hurt, and one hurt can be shattered and sprinkled over a thousand days. It is silent and elusive, refusing to be dammed and dripped out day by day; it swirls through the mind while an entire lifetime can ride like foam on the deceptive, transparent waves and get sprayed onto the consciousness at ragged, unexpected intervals.

IV

Mattie got up Sunday morning to the usual banging and howling in the house on weekends. Miss Eva was in the kitchen fighting with the children.

"Grandma, Basil broke my crayon. See, he bit it right in

half—and on purpose!" Lucielia wailed.

"Basil, you little red devil, come here! Can't I cook breakfast in peace?"

"But, Miss Eva, Ciel took my coloring book and she tore all the pages."

"I did not," Ciel protested, and kicked him.

Basil began crying.

"Why, you evil, narrow-tailed heifer. I'll break your neck!" And she smacked Ciel on the behind with her wooden cooking spoon.

Basil stopped crying instantly in order to enjoy Ciel's punishment. "Goody, goody." He stuck out his tongue at her.

"Goody, goody, on you, Mister," Miss Eva went after him with the spoon, "I ain't forgot you broke my china poodle this morning."

Basil ducked under the table, knowing she wouldn't be able to bend and reach him.

"Want me to get him for you, Grandma?" Ciel offered, trying to get back into her good graces.

"No, I just want you both out of my kitchen. Out! Out!" She banged on the table with the spoon.

Mattie stood yawning in the kitchen door. "Can't there be just one morning of peace and quiet in this house—just one?" Ciel and Basil both ran to her, each trying to outshout the other about their various injustices. "I don't want to hear it," Mattie sighed. "It's too early for this nonsense. Now go wash up for breakfast—you're still in pajamas."

"Didn't you hear her? Now, get!" Miss Eva shouted and raised her spoon.

The children ran upstairs. Eva smiled behind their backs and turned toward the stove.

"Well, good morning," Mattie said, and poured herself a cup of coffee.

" 'Tain't natural, just 'tain't natural," Miss Eva grumbled at the stove.

"They're only children, Miss Eva. All children are like that."

"I ain't talking about them children, I'm talking 'bout you. You done spent another weekend holed up in this house and ain't gone out nowhere."

"Now that's not true. Friday night I went to choir practice, and Saturday I took Basil to get a pair of shoes and then took him and Ciel to the zoo. And last night I even went to a double feature at the Century, which is why I overslept this morning. That only leaves Sunday morning, Miss Eva, and there's church today, and then I gotta go back to work tomorrow. So I don't know what you're talkin' about."

"What I'm talkin' 'bout is that I ain't heard you mention no man involved in all them exciting goings-on in your life—church and children and work. It ain't natural for a young woman like you to live that way. I can't remember the last time no man come by to take you out."

Mattie couldn't remember either. There had been a bus ride with a foreman in the shipping department at her job, and she had gone out a few times with one of the ushers in her church—but that was last spring, or was it last winter?

"Humph." Mattie shrugged her shoulders and sipped her coffee. "I've been so busy, I guess I haven't noticed. It has been a long time, but so what? I've got my hands full raising my son."

"Children get raised overnight, Mattie. Then what you got? I should know. I raised seven and four of my grand and they all gone except Ciel. But I'm an old woman, my life's most over. That ain't no excuse for you. Why, by the time I was your age, I was on my second husband, and you still slow about gettin' the first."

"Well, Miss Eva, I'd have to had started twenty years ago to beat your record," Mattie kidded.

"I ain't making no joke, child." And her watery eyes clouded over as she stared at the younger woman. Mattie knew that look well. The old woman wanted a confrontation and would not be budged. "Ain't you ever had no needs in that direction? No young woman wants an empty bed, year in and year out."

Mattie felt the blood rushing to her face under Miss Eva's open stare. She took a few sips of coffee to give herself time to think. Why didn't she ever feel that way? Was there really something wrong with her? The answers were beyond her at that moment, but Miss Eva was waiting, and she had to say something.

"My bed hasn't been empty since Basil was born," she said lightly, "and I don't think anyone but me would put up with the way that boy kicks in his sleep."

As soon as the words were out, she regretted them. This was an ancient battle between the two women.

"Basil needs a bed of his own. I been telling you that for years."

"He's afraid of the dark. You know that."

"Most children are afraid at first, but they get used to it."

"I'm not gonna have my child screaming his head off all night just to please you. He's still a baby, he doesn't like sleeping alone, and that's it!" she said through clenched teeth.

"Five years old ain't no baby," Miss Eva said. And then she added mildly, "You sure it's Basil who don't want to sleep alone?"

The gentle pity in the faded blue eyes robbed Mattie of the angry accusations she wanted to fling at the old woman for making her feel ashamed. Shame for what? For loving her son, wanting to protect him from his invisible phantoms that lay crouching in the dark? No, those pitying eyes had slid into her unconscious like a blue laser and exposed secrets that Mattie had buried from her own self. They had crept between her sheets and knew that her body had hungered at moments, had felt the need for a filling and caressing of inner spaces. But in those restless moments she had turned toward her manchild and let the soft, sleeping flesh and the thought of all that he was and would be draw those yearnings onto the edge of her lips and the tips of her fingers. And she could not sleep until she released those congested feelings by stroking his moist forehead and planting a kiss there. A mother's kiss for a sleeping child. And this old woman's freakish blue eyes had turned it into something to make her ashamed.

She wanted to get up from the table and spit into those eyes, beat them sightless—those that had befriended her, kept her baby from sharp objects and steep stairs while she worked, wept with her over the death of her parents—she wanted them crushed under her fists for daring to make her ashamed of loving her son.

"I don't have to take this," Mattie stammered defensively. "Just because we stay in your house don't give you a right to tell me how to raise my child. I'm a boarder here, or at least I would be if you'd let me pay you. Just tell me how much I owe you, and I'll pay up and be out before the week's over."

"I ain't decided yet."

"You been saying that for five years!" Mattie was frustrated.

"And you been movin' every time I mention anything about that little spoiled nigger of yours. You still saving my rent money in the bank, ain't you?"

"Of course." Mattie had religiously put aside money every month, and her account had grown quite large.

"Good, you'll be using it soon enough for new clothes for my funeral. That is, if you plan on coming?"

Mattie looked at Miss Eva's stooped back and the wrinkled yellow neck with grizzled wisps of hair lying on it, and small needles of repentance began to stab at her heart. She would be gone soon, and Mattie didn't want to imagine facing the loss of another mother.

"You're a crafty old woman. You always try to win an argument by talkin' about some funeral. You're too ornery to die, and you know it."

Miss Eva chuckled. "Some folks do say that. To tell you the truth, I had planned on stayin' till I'm a hundred."

Please do, Mattie thought sadly, and then said aloud, "No, I couldn't bear you that long—maybe till ninety-nine and a half."

They smiled at each other and silently agreed to put the argument to rest.

The children came running into the kitchen, scrubbed and penitent. "Let me check those ears," Mattie said to Ciel and Basil.

She was about to send him back upstairs to wash his when he put his arms around her neck and said, "Mama, I forgot to kiss you hello this morning." Basil knew he would win his reprieve this way. Miss Eva knew it, too, but she said nothing as she slung the oatmeal into their bowls and slowly shook her head.

Mattie was aware of only the joy that these unsolicited acts of tenderness gave her. She watched him eating his oatmeal, intent on each mouthful that he swallowed because it was keeping her son alive. It was moving through his blood and creating skin cells and hair cells and new muscles that would eventually uncurl and multiply and stretch the skin on his upper arms and thighs, elongate the plump legs that only reached the top rung of his chair. And when they had reached the second rung, Miss Eva would be dead. Her children would have descended upon the beautiful house and stripped it of all that was valuable and sold the rest to Mattie. Her parents would have carried away a screaming Ciel, and as Mattie would look around the gutted house, she'd know why the old yellow woman had made her save her money. She had wanted her spirit to remain in this house through the memory of someone who was capable of loving it as she had. While Basil's legs pushed down toward the third rung, Mattie would be working two jobs to carry the mortgage on the house. Her son must have room to grow in, a yard to run in, a decent place to bring his friends. Her own spirit must one day have a place to rest because the body could not, as it pushed and struggled to make all around them safe and comfortable. It would all be for him and those to come from the long, muscular thighs of him who sat opposite her at the table.

Mattie looked at the man who was gulping coffee and

shoveling oatmeal into his mouth. "Why you eating so fast? You'll choke."

"I got some place to go."

"It's Sunday, Basil. You been runnin' all weekend. I thought you were gonna stay home and help me with the yard."

"Look, I'm only going out for a few minutes. I told you I'll cut the grass, and I will, so stop hassling me."

Mattie remained silent because she didn't want to argue with him while he ate. He'd had a nervous stomach all his life, and she didn't want him to get cramps or run out of the house, refusing to eat at all. She doubted that she would see him anymore that day, and she wanted to be certain he got at least one decent meal.

"All right, you want more toast or coffee?" she offered, as way of apology.

He really didn't, but he let her fix him another cup to show that he was no longer annoyed. He thanked her by remaining to finish his breakfast.

"Okay, I'll see you in a while," he said, and pushed his chair back. "Hey, could you lend me a coupla dollars to get some gas for the car?" He saw that she had opened her mouth to refuse and went on, "I don't want it for today but tomorrow, I gotta go looking for another job. I don't pick up my check from the last place until Thursday, and I don't wanna waste four days sitting around here doing nothing." He bent down and whispered in her ear, "You know I'm not the kind of guy to hang around and let a woman support him." Seeing her smile, he straightened up and said, "But I would make a good pimp, wouldn't I, Mama?" And he pantomimed putting on a cocked hat and strutted in the middle of the floor.

Mattie laughed and openly scorned his foolish antics while inwardly admitting that he had to be considered attractive by many women. Basil looked exactly like his father, but the clean, naturally curved lines of Butch's mouth seemed transformed into a mild sullenness when placed on Basil's face. His clear brown eyes were heavily lashed, and many young women had discovered just one heartbeat too late that his slightly drooping eyelids were not mirrors of boyish seductiveness but hardened apathy.

Mattie had never met any of Basil's girlfriends, and he rarely mentioned them. She thought about this as she gave him the money and watched him leave the house. She cleared off the breakfast dishes, and it suddenly came to her that she hadn't met many of his male friends, either. Where was he going? She truly didn't know, and it had come to be understood that she was not to ask. How long had it been that way? Surely it had happened within moments. It seemed that only hours ago he had been the child who could hug her neck and talk himself out of a spanking, who had brought home crayoned valentines, and had cried when she went to her second job. So then, who was this stranger who had done away with her little boy and left her with no one and so alone?

Mattie pondered this as her hands plunged into the soapy dishwater, and she mechanically washed bowls and silverware. She tried to recapture the years and hold them up for inspection, so she could pinpoint the transformation, but they slipped through her fingers and slid down the dishes, hidden under the iridescent bubbles that broke with the slightest movement of her hand. She quickly saw that it was an impossible task and abandoned the effort. He had grown up, that was all. She looked up from the sink and gasped as she caught her reflection in the windowpane—but when had she grown old?

Any possible answer had disappeared down the drain with the used dishwater, and she watched it go without regret and scoured the porcelain until it shone. She changed the freshly starched kitchen curtains and rewaxed the tiles. She went through the house vacuuming clean carpets and dusting spotless tables—these were the testimony to her lost years. There was a need to touch and smell and see that it was all in place. It would always be there to comfort and affirm when she would have nothing else.

She could not find the little boy whom this had all been for, but she found an old cut-glass bowl that she washed and polished and filled with autumn flowers from her yard. She put the bowl on a windowsill in her sun porch, and, exhausted, sat among the huge vines and plants, watching the fading sun dissolve into the prismed edges of the bowl. She loved this room above all the others—a place to see things grow. And she had watched and coaxed and nurtured the greenery about her. Miss Eva's presence was there in the few pieces of china bric-a-brac that Mattie had saved over the years. And it was here that she would come and sit when there was a problem or some complex decision to be made. She felt guilty about missing church that day, but if God were everywhere, surely He was here among so much natural beauty and peace. So Mattie sat there and prayed, but sometimes her supplications for comfort were to the wisdom of a yellow, blue-eyed spirit who had foreseen this day and had tried to warn her.

Mattie sat there for hours, and still Basil did not come. She looked through the windows at the long grass and decided to cut it the next day after work, if her back didn't bother her too much. It was becoming more difficult each year to keep up the house alone. She got up from the couch stiffly and climbed the steps toward her bedroom.

Her house slippers scraped the edges of the steps. Irresponsible, his counselors had said in school. High-natured, she had replied in her heart. Hadn't he said that they were always picking on him; everyone had been against him, except her. She had been the refuge when he ran from school to school, job to job. They wanted too much. She had been so proud that he always turned to her—fled to her when he accused them of demanding the impossible. "Irresponsible"—the word whispered on the soft carpet as her feet dragged up the dark stairs. She had demanded nothing all these years, never doubting that he would be there when needed. She had carefully pruned his spirit to rest only in the enclaves of her will, and she had willed so little that he had been tempted to return again and again over the last thirty years because his just being had been enough to satisfy her needs. But now her back was tightening in the mornings, and her grass was growing wild and ragged over the walkway while she pulled herself painfully up the stairs, alone.

V

Mattie slept lightly that night, and she dreamed that she was running and hiding from something among tall bamboo stalks and monstrously tangled weeds. She was terribly hungry and mysteriously frightened of the invisible thing that was searching for her. She had a piece of sugar cane in her hand, and she wedged it into her mouth and chewed, trying to stop the burning hunger in her stomach. She was desperately trying to chew the cane before this stalking thing found her. She sensed it coming closer through the tall grass, its heavy footsteps pounding in her ears, timed with the beating of her heart. She screamed as it parted the grass that was covering her. It was Butch. He was smiling and glowing, and his eyes were blue and spinning crazily in their sockets. He tried to pry open her mouth and scrape out the mashed wad of sugar cane. He grabbed her by the throat to keep the saliva from being swallowed, and she opened her mouth and screamed and screamed—shrill notes that vibrated in her ears and sent terrible pains shooting into her head.

Mattie woke up trembling and lay dazed among the tangled bedcovers. She covered her ears to block out the shrill screams that continued to echo through her head. After a moment she realized that the noise was coming from the telephone on her nightstand. Her heart was still pounding as she blindly groped for the phone.

"Yes?"

"Mama, it's me."

She held the hard plastic receiver to her ear and tried to make sense out of the electrical impulses that were forming

words—strange words that could have no possible association with the voice on the other end.

A bar. A woman. A fight. A booking.

"Basil?" Surely this voice was Basil's.

Fingerprints. Manslaughter. Lawyer.

Mattie sat up in bed, gripped the receiver, and tried to
follow these new words as they came flying out of the receiver and spun bizarre patterns in her head. She was frantically trying to link them into sentences, phrases—anything
that she could place within her world—but it all made no
sense.

"What are you talking about?" she yelled into the phone.

". . . And the son-of-a-bitches beat me up! They beat me
up, Mama!" And the voice began to cry.

This she understood. Conditioned by years of instinctual
response to his tears, Mattie's head cleared immediately, and
she jumped out of bed.

"Who beat you up? Where are you?"

As the late November winds cut across her legs and blew
under her coat, Mattie shivered violently and realized that
she had rushed from the house without any slip or stockings.
She pulled her tweed coat closer to her neck to cut off the
wind and stop her body from trembling with cold, and moved
on toward the police precinct. The brick and glass building
threw out a ghostly light against the thin morning air. She
paused a moment to catch her breath before the iron lettering engraved over the door and then pushed the slanted
metal bar and went in.

The warm air in the room smelled like stale ink and dried
saliva. There was nothing in it but a few scarred wooden
benches and rows of closed smoked-glass doors. She had expected to see Basil, and his absence terrified her. She angrily approached the policeman at the desk.

They had her son. Where was her son?
Who was her son? the tired face queried.

Basil Michael. He had just called her from here. They had beat him up and hidden him away behind one of those doors. He was hurt, and she demanded to know why. She had come to take him home.

The tired face sighed, flipped slowly through a clipboard of papers, and read one of them to her. No one had beat up her son; he had resisted arrest, and the officers involved had used due force to restrain the suspect. He was being held for involuntary manslaughter and assaulting a peace officer. He would be arraigned in Penal Court IVA, tomorrow after-noon.

More new words—cold words that meant only one thing to her—she could not get to Basil, and he was somewhere in this building and he needed her. How dare they do this?

Where was her son? She had to see her son.
She could see him tomorrow, before the arraignment.
She wanted to see him now. Maybe they had hit him in the stomach. He had a weak stomach and might need a doc-tor. She wasn't leaving until she saw her son.

Sergeant Manchester massaged the tightness between his sleepy eyes and looked wearily at the desperate bewilder-ment that stood in front of him. Any pity that he might have felt for this old black woman lay buried under the memory of a hundred such faces on countless other mornings like this one. It never ended—someone's somebody—all persistently filed in to bruise their heads upon the rigid walls of due process.

"Lady," he said with a tone of genuine sadness, "there's a man laying in the morgue because of an argument in a bar with your son, and a police officer has a broken wrist. Do you understand? Now if you want to help him, I suggest that you get a lawyer, or come back and talk to the public defender in the afternoon. That would be the best thing that

46

you could do for him right now. Okay? Please, go home. Here are the regulations and visiting hours." And he bent his head back over his reports.

Mattie looked at the inked markings on the slip of paper that dictated the conditions for her ever touching Basil again. She studied the fine lines and loops, commas and periods that had come between them, and they etched themselves into her mind. She crumpled the paper and dropped it on the floor.

"Thank you," she said, turned, and walked toward the door.

Sergeant Manchester glanced at her back, saw the paper on the floor, and called to her. "Lady, you forgot the visiting hours."

"No, I didn't," she said, without turning around, and went through the door.

There was no need to worry, the bifocals kept telling her later that day, after seeing Basil. Acquittal was certain. This was his first major offense, and the other party had provoked the fight. There were several witnesses to this and to the fact that death had occurred when the other party's head hit the edge of the bar. The assault on the police officer would be a bit sticky, but the court was certain to suspend the sentence when it was argued that the defendant was in an unduly agitated state of mind. It would really be an easy case, should take two days at the most, once it's brought to trial. When would that be? The date would be set tomorrow at the arraignment. Of course, she could go in now and see her son. And please, there was no need to worry.

Cecil Garvin pulled off his glasses and tapped the handle against his teeth as he thoughtfully watched Mattie's retreating back. He wondered why she hadn't let the public defender take care of such a simple case. He would be receiving a huge fee for something that wouldn't even require a trial by jury if it was in the next county. Well, he sighed, and put his glasses back on. Thank God for ignorance of the law and frantic mothers.

"Baby, there ain't nothing to worry about," she told Basil as she stroked his hand, trying to calm the frightened look in his eyes. "I went to Reverend Kelly, and he referred me to a good criminal lawyer. Now he said it would be all right, and it will."

"When am I getting out of here? That's what I want to know." And he snatched his hand away and nervously drummed it on the table.

"Tomorrow, after some kind of hearing, they'll tell us when you'll go to trial."

"I don't understand this!" he exploded. "Why should there be a trial? It was an accident! And that guy was picking on me over some broad. I don't even know his name."

"I know, honey, but a man is dead, and there's gotta be some kind of proceeding about it."

"Well, he's better off than me. This place is a hellhole, and see what those bastards did to my face."

Mattie winced as she forced herself to stare at his bruised face. "They said you resisted arrest, Basil, and broke a policeman's wrist," she said softly.

"So what!" He glared at her. "They wanted to put me in jail for something that wasn't my fault. They had no right to do this to me, and now you're sticking up for them."

"Oh, Basil," Mattie sighed, suddenly feeling the strain of the last twelve hours, "I ain't sticking up for nobody, but we gotta face what happened so we can see our way clear from this."

"It's not 'we,' Mama, it's me. I'm stuck in here—not you. It's filthy and smelly, and I even heard rats under my bed last night."

Mattie's stomach knotted into tiny spasms.

"So when am I leaving?"

"Tomorrow at the hearing, when they tell us the bail, I'll put it up and then you can get out."

"Can't you give them the bail money today? I can't spend another night in this place."

"Basil, there's nothing I can do today. We have to wait." Mattie pressed a trembling hand to her eyes to hold back the tears. She had never felt so impotent in her life. There was no way she could fight the tiny inked markings that now controlled their lives. She would give anything to remove him from this horrible place—didn't he know that? But those blue loops, commas, and periods had tied her hands.

"Okay, fine. If you can't, you can't," he said bitterly, and got up from his chair.

"Honey, we still got time, don't you want to sit and talk?"

"There's nothing left to talk about, Mama, unless you wanna hear about the broken toilets with three-day-old shit or the bedbugs that have ate up my back or the greasy food I keep throwing up. Other than that, I got nothing to say to you."

He left Mattie sitting there, understanding his frustration but wishing he had chosen a kinder way of hurting her, by just hitting her in the face.

The judge set bail the next day, and Basil was given an early trial date. Cecil Garvin tried to appeal the bail, but the court denied his plea.

"I'm sorry, Mrs. Michael, it's the best I could do. There's no need, really, to try and raise so much money. The case goes to trial in only two weeks, and it won't be a complicated proceeding. I've talked to the district attorney, and they won't push too heavily on the assault charge if we drop the implications of undue force in the arrest. So it's going to work out well for all the parties involved. And your son will be free in less than fifteen days."

"I still want to put up the bail," Mattie said.

Garvin looked worried. "It's a great deal of money, Mrs.

Michael, and you don't have the ready assets for something like that."

"I've got my house; it's mine and paid for. Can't I put that up for bail?"

"Well, yes, but you do understand that bail is only posted to insure that the defendant appears for trial. If they don't appear, the court issues a bench warrant for the truant party and you forfeit your bond. You do understand that?"

"I understand."

The lawyer looked thoughtfully over at Basil. "It's only a matter of two weeks, Mrs. Michael. Some defendants spend months waiting for trial. Perhaps you should reconsider."

Mattie stared at him, and she thought about the blonde girl in the silver frame on his desk. "If it was your daughter locked up in a place like that," she said angrily, "could you stand there and say the same thing?"

His face reddened, and he stammered for a moment. "That's not what I mean, Mrs. Michael. It's just that with some people it's better to . . . well, it's up to you. It is your son, after all. Come along, and I'll give you the necessary papers to take to a bonding company."

The snow fell early that year. When Basil and Mattie left the precinct, the wide soft flakes were floating in gentle layers on the November air. Basil reached out and tried to grab one to give her, and he laughed as it melted in his hand.

"Remember how I used to cry when I tried to bring you a snowflake and it always disappeared?" He held his face up to the sky and let the snow fall on his closed lids. "Oh, God, Mama, isn't it beautiful?"

"Beautiful? You always hated the snow."

"Not now, it's wonderful. It's out here and free, like I am. I love it!" And he wrapped his arms around himself.

Mattie's insides expanded to take in his joy.

"And I love you, Mama." He put his arm around her shoulder and squeezed. "Thank you."

Mattie sucked her teeth and playfully shoved him away. "Thank me for what? Boy, go on and get the car before I catch my death of cold in all this beautiful snow of yours."

Mattie watched him as he moved through the parking lot almost singing, and she took in his happiness and made it her own just as she'd done with every emotion that had ever claimed him. She took in the sweetness of his freedom and let it roll around her tongue, while she savored its fragrant juices and allowed the syrupy fluid to coat her mouth and drip slowly down her throat.

She feasted on this sweetness during the next two weeks. Basil had been returned to her, and she reveled in his presence. He drove her to work in the mornings and would often be waiting when she got off. They cleaned the yard together and covered her shrubbery with burlap. They rearranged furniture and straightened the attic, and he even washed windows for her—a chore he had hated from childhood. There was no end to the things he did for her, and he stayed close to home. It was so good to have a nice home to come to, he told her. And she grew full from this nectar and allowed herself to dream again of the wife he would bring home and the grandchildren who would keep her spirit there.

The lawyer called at the end of the second week to remind them of the court appointment, and Basil grew irritable. He told her he hated the thought of that place. He had tried to pretend that it didn't exist, and he had been so happy. Now this. What if something went wrong and they kept him again? You couldn't trust those honky lawyers—what did they care about him? Those people in that bar weren't friends of his— what if they changed their stories? What if the girl hated him now and decided to lie? He remembered the way she had screamed over the dead man's body. Yes, she would lie to get back at him. He knew it.

"I'll blow my brains out before I spend my life in jail," he said to Mattie while driving her to work.

"Basil, stop talkin' stupidness!" Her voice was sharp. She had not been able to sleep well the last two nights, lying and listening to him pacing around in his room. "I've been hearing nothing but nonsense the last coupla days, and I'm sick of it."

"Nonsense!" He swung his head around.

"Yes, damned nonsense! You ain't going to jail 'cause you ain't done nothing to go to jail for. We go to court Tuesday; they'll give all the evidence, and you'll be clear. That's all there is to it. The lawyer said so, and he should know."

"Mama, he'll say anything to get your money. If someone offered him a nickel more than you paid, he'd throw me in jail personally and swallow the key. You don't know them like I do, and you don't know what it's like in those cells. And they'll send me to a worse place than some county jail." He looked at her sorrowfully. "I couldn't stand it, Mama. I just couldn't."

Mattie sighed, turned her head from him, and looked out the window. There was nothing to say. Whatever was lacking within him that made it impossible to confront the difficulties of life could not be supplied with words. She saw it now. There was a void in his being that had been padded and cushioned over the years, and now that covering had grown impregnable. She bit on her bottom lip and swallowed back a sob. God had given her what she prayed for—a little boy who would always need her.

She felt him looking at her turned head from time to time and knew he was puzzled by her silence. He was waiting to be coaxed and petted into a lighter mood, but she forced herself to keep staring out the window. When the car pulled up to her job, she mumbled a good-bye and reached for the latch. Basil grabbed her hand, leaned over, and kissed her cheek.

"Good-bye, Mama."

She was touched by the gentleness in his caress and immediately repentant of her attitude in the car. During the day she resolved to make amends to him. After all, he was under a great deal of pressure, and it wasn't fair that he bear it alone. Was it so wrong that he seemed to need her constant support? Had he not been trained to expect it? And he had been trying so hard those last two weeks; she couldn't let him down now. She would go home and make him a special dinner—creamed chicken with rice—he always loved that. Then they would sit and talk, and she would tell him, once again, or as many times as needed, that it was going to be all right.

Basil wasn't waiting for Mattie when she finished work, so she took the bus home and stopped by the store to pick up the things she needed for his dinner. She walked up the street and saw that his car wasn't parked out front and the house was dark. She stood for a moment by the front gate, first looking at the space where the car should be and then at the unlit windows. Normally she would have gone through the front door, taken off her coat, and hung it in the front hall closet. Tonight she entered the house through the back door that led straight into the kitchen. She took off her coat and laid it on one of the kitchen chairs. There was an extra jacket of his in the front hall closet that would not be there.

She washed her hands at the sink and immediately started to cut up the chicken and peel and slice vegetables. Her feet were beginning to ache, but her house slippers were in the living room, under a table where his portable radio would not be, so she limped around her kitchen while finishing his dinner. She let the water run in the sink longer than necessary and dropped her knife and set the pots on the stove with a fraction of extra force. She made as much noise as she could to ward off the stillness of the upstairs bedroom that kept trying to creep into her kitchen, carrying empty drawers and closets, a vacant space where a suitcase had lain, missing toothpaste. She banged pot lids and beat sauces in aluminum bowls until her arms were tired. She watched and fussed over his dinner, opening and closing the oven door a dozen times—anything to keep back the stillness until he would drive up in his car, say he had come to his senses, sit down and eat her creamed chicken, save a lifetime of work lying in the bricks of her home.

The vegetables were done, the chicken almost burnt, and the biscuits had to come out of the oven. She turned off the gas jets, opened the oven door, and banged the pan of biscuits onto the counter top. She looked frantically at the creeping shadows over her kitchen door and rushed to the cabinet and took out plates and silverware. She slammed the cabinet shut and slowly and noisily set the table for two. She looked pleadingly around the kitchen, but there was nothing left to be done. So she pulled out the kitchen chair, letting the metal legs drag across the tiles. Trembling, she sat down, put her head in her hands, and waited for the patient and crouching stillness just beyond the kitchen door.

A hand touched her shoulder, and Mattie gave a small cry.
"Didn't mean to startle you, mam, but it's snowing pretty bad, and we gotta move this stuff upstairs. Would you please go up and unlock the door?"
At first Mattie looked vacantly into the face of the man, and then her mind snapped into place from its long stretch over time. The cab had just backed out of Brewster Place, and she watched it turn down the avenue and drive away. Her eyes trailed slowly along the cracked stoops and snow-filled gutters until they came to her building. She glanced at the wall and, with an inner sigh, remembered her plants again.
The mover who had addressed her was staring at her uncomfortably.
"Oh, yes, I'm sorry," she said disconcertedly. "I have the keys right here, don't I?" And she opened her pocketbook and started searching for them.
The two men looked at each other, and one shrugged his shoulders and pointed his finger toward his head.
Mattie grasped the cold metal key in one hand and put the other on the iron railing and climbed the stoop to the front entrance. As she opened the door and entered the dingy hallway, a snowflake caught in her collar, melted, and rolled down her back like a frozen tear.

ETTA MAE
JOHNSON

*The unpainted walls of the long rectangular room were soaked
with the smell of greasy chicken and warm, headless beer.
The brown and pink faces floated above the trails of used
cigarette smoke like bodiless carnival balloons. The plump
yellow woman with white gardenias pinned to the side of her
head stood with her back pressed against the peeling sides of
the baby grand and tried to pierce the bloated hum in the
room with her thin scratchy voice. Undisturbed that she remained for the most part ignored, she motioned for the
piano player to begin.*

*It wasn't the music or the words or the woman that took
that room by its throat until it gasped for air—it was the
pain. There was a young southern girl, Etta Johnson, pushed
up in a corner table, and she never forgot. The music, the
woman, the words.*

> I love my man
> I'm a lie if I say I don't
> I love my man
> I'm a lie if I say I don't
> But I'll quit my man
> I'm a lie if I say I won't
>
> My man wouldn't give me no breakfast
> Wouldn't give me no dinner
> Squawked about my supper
> Then he put me out of doors

Had the nerve to lay
A matchbox to my clothes
I didn't have so many
But I had a long, long, way to go

Children bloomed on Brewster Place during July and August with their colorful shorts and tops plastered against gold, ebony, and nut-brown legs and arms; they decorated the street, rivaling the geraniums and ivy found on the manicured boulevard downtown. The summer heat seemed to draw the people from their cramped apartments onto the stoops, as it drew the tiny drops of perspiration from their foreheads and backs.

The apple-green Cadillac with the white vinyl roof and Florida plates turned into Brewster like a greased cobra. Since Etta had stopped at a Mobil station three blocks away to wash off the evidence of a hot, dusty 1200-mile odyssey home, the chrome caught the rays of the high afternoon sun and flung them back into its face. She had chosen her time well.

The children, free from the conditioned restraints of their older counterparts, ran along the sidewalks flanking this curious, slow-moving addition to their world. Every eye on the block, either openly or covertly, was on the door of the car when it opened. They were rewarded by the appearance of a pair of white leather sandals attached to narrow ankles and slightly bowed, shapely legs. The willow-green sundress, only ten minutes old on the short chestnut woman, clung to a body that had finished a close second in its race with time. Large two-toned sunglasses hid the weariness that had defied the freshly applied mascara and burnt-ivory shadow. After taking twice the time needed to stretch herself, she reached into the back seat of the car and pulled out her plastic clothes bag and Billie Holiday albums.

The children's curiosity reached the end of its short life span, and they drifted back to their various games. The adults sucked their teeth in disappointment, and the more envious felt self-righteousness twist the corners of their mouths. It was only Etta. Looked like she'd done all right by herself—this time around.

Slowly she carried herself across the street—head high and eyes fixed unwaveringly on her destination. The half-dozen albums were clutched in front of her chest like cardboard armor.

> There ain't nothing I ever do
> Or nothing I ever say
> That folks don't criticize me
> But I'm going to do
> Just what I want to, anyway
> And don't care just what people say
> If I should take a notion
> To jump into the ocean
> Ain't nobody's business if I do . . .

Any who bothered to greet her never used her first name. No one called Etta Mae "Etta," except in their minds; and when they spoke to each other about her, it was Etta Johnson; but when they addressed her directly, it was always Miss Johnson. This baffled her because she knew what they thought about her, and she'd always call them by their first names and invited them to do the same with her. But after a few awkward attempts, they'd fall back into the pattern they were somehow comfortable with. Etta didn't know if this was to keep the distance on her side or theirs, but it was there. And she had learned to tread through these alien undercurrents so well that to a casual observer she had mastered the ancient secret of walking on water.

Mattie sat in her frayed brocade armchair, pushed up to the front window, and watched her friend's brave approach through the dusty screen. Still toting around them oversized records, she thought. That woman is a puzzlement.

Mattie rose to open the door so Etta wouldn't have to

struggle to knock with her arms full. "Lord, child, thank you," she gushed, out of breath. "The younger I get, the higher those steps seem to stretch."

She dumped her load on the sofa and swept off her sunglasses. She breathed deeply of the freedom she found in Mattie's presence. Here she had no choice but to be herself. The carefully erected decoys she was constantly shuffling and changing to fit the situation were of no use here. Etta and Mattie went way back, a singular term that claimed co-knowledge of all the important events in their lives and almost all of the unimportant ones. And by rights of this possession, it tolerated no secrets.

"Sit on down and take a breather. Must have been a hard trip. When you first said you were coming, I didn't expect you to be driving."

"To tell the truth, I didn't expect it myself, Mattie. But Simeon got very ornery when I said I was heading home, and he refused to give me the money he'd promised for my plane fare. So I said, just give me half and I'll take the train. Well, he wasn't gonna even do that. And Mattie, you know I'll be damned if I was coming into this city on a raggedy old Greyhound. So one night he was by my place all drunk up and snoring, and as kindly as you please, I took the car keys and registration and so here I am."

"My God, woman! You stole the man's car?"

"Stole—nothing. He owes me that and then some."

"Yeah, but the police don't wanna hear that. It's a wonder the highway patrol ain't stopped you before now."

"They ain't stopped me because Simeon didn't report it."

"How you know that?"

"His wife's daddy is the sheriff of that county." Laughter hung dangerously on the edge of the two women's eyes and lips.

"Yeah, but he could say you picked his pockets."

Etta went to her clothes bag and pulled out a pair of pink and red monogrammed shorts. "I'd have to be a damned good pickpocket to get away with all this." The laughter lost

58

its weak hold on their mouths and went bouncing crazily
against the walls of the living room.

Them that's got, shall get
Them that's not, shall lose
So the Bible says
And it still is news

Each time the laughter would try to lie still, the two
women would look at each other and send it hurling between them, once again.

Mama may have
Papa may have
But God bless the child
That's got his own
That's got his own

"Lord, Tut, you're a caution." Mattie wiped the tears off
her cheeks with the back of a huge dark hand.

Etta was unable to count the years that had passed since
she had heard someone call her that. Look a' that baby gal
strutting around here like a bantam. You think she'd be the
wife of King Tut. The name had stayed because she never
lost the walk. The washed-out grime and red mud of back-
woods Rock Vale, Tennessee, might wrap itself around her
bare feet and coat the back of her strong fleshy legs, but Etta
always had her shoulders flung behind her collarbone and
her chin thrust toward the horizon that came to mean everything Rock Vale did not.

Etta spent her teenage years in constant trouble. Rock Vale
had no place for a black woman who was not only unwilling
to play by the rules, but whose spirit challenged the very
right of the game to exist. The whites in Rock Vale were
painfully reminded of this rebellion when she looked them
straight in the face while putting in her father's order at the
dry goods store, when she reserved her sirs and mams for

those she thought deserving, and when she smiled only if
pleased, regardless of whose presence she was in. That Johnson gal wasn't being an uppity nigger, as talk had it; she was
just being herself.

Southern trees bear strange fruit
Blood on the leaves and blood at the root
Black bodies swinging
In the southern breeze
Strange fruit hanging
From the poplar trees

But Rutherford County wasn't ready for Etta's blooming
independence, and so she left one rainy summer night about
three hours ahead of dawn and Johnny Brick's furious pur-
suing relatives. Mattie wrote and told her they had waited
in ambush for two days on the county line, and then had
returned and burned down her father's barn. The sheriff told
Mr. Johnson that he had gotten off mighty light—considering. Mr. Johnson thought so, too. After reading Mattie's letter, Etta was sorry she hadn't killed the horny white bastard
when she had the chance.

Rock Vale had followed her to Memphis, Detroit, Chicago, and even to New York. Etta soon found out that America wasn't ready for her yet—not in 1937. And so along with
the countless other disillusioned, restless children of Ham
with so much to give and nowhere to give it, she took her
talents to the street. And she learned to get over, to hook
herself to any promising rising black star, and when he burnt
out, she found another.

Her youth had ebbed away quickly under the steady pressure of the changing times, but she was existing as she always had. Even if someone had bothered to stop and tell
her that the universe had expanded for her, just an inch, she
wouldn't have known how to shine alone.

Etta and Mattie had taken totally different roads that with
all of their deceptive winding had both ended up on Brew-

ster Place. Their laughter now drew them into a conspirato-
rial circle against all the Simeons outside of that dead-end
street, and it didn't stop until they were both weak from the
tears that flowed down their faces.

"So," Mattie said, blowing her nose on a large cotton
handkerchief, "trusting you stay out of jail, what you plan on
doing now?"

"Child, I couldn't tell you." Etta dropped back down on
the couch. "I should be able to get a coupla thousand for the
car to tide me over till another business opportunity comes
along."

Mattie raised one eyebrow just a whisper of an inch. "Ain't
it time you got yourself a regular job? These last few years
them *business opportunities* been fewer and farther between."

Etta sucked her small white teeth. "A job doing what?
Come on, Mattie, what kind of experience I got? Six months
here, three there. I oughta find me a good man and settle
down to live quiet in my old age." She combed her fingers
confidently through the thick sandy hair that only needed
slight tinting at the roots and mentally gave herself another
fifteen years before she had to worry about this ultimate
fate.

Mattie, watching the creeping tiredness in her eyes, gave
her five. "You done met a few promising ones along the way,
Etta."

"No, honey, it just seemed so. Let's face it, Mattie. All
the good men are either dead or waiting to be born."

"Why don't you come to meeting with me tonight. There's
a few settle-minded men in our church, some widowers and
such. And a little prayer wouldn't hurt your soul one bit."

"I'll thank you to leave my soul well alone, Mattie Michael. And if your church is so full of upright Christian
men, why you ain't snagged one yet?"

"Etta, I done banked them fires a long time ago, but seeing
that you still keeping up steam . . ." Her eyes were full of
playful kindness.

"Just barely, Mattie, just barely."

And laughter rolled inside of 2E, once again.

"Etta, Etta Mae!" Mattie banged on the bathroom door. "Come on out now. You making me late for the meeting."

"Just another second, Mattie. The church ain't gonna walk away."

"Lord," Mattie grumbled, "she ain't bigger than a minute, so it shouldn't take more than that to get ready."

Etta came out of the bathroom in an exaggerated rush. "My, my, you the most impatient Christian I know."

"Probably, the only Christian you know." Mattie refused to be humored as she bent to gather up her sweater and purse. She turned and was stunned with a barrage of colors. A huge white straw hat reigned over layers of gold and pearl beads draped over too much bosom and too little dress. "You plan on dazzling the Lord, Etta?"

"Well, honey," Etta said, looking down the back of her stocking leg to double-check for runs, "last I heard, He wasn't available. You got more recent news?"

"Um, um, um." Mattie pressed her lips together and shook her head slowly to swallow down the laughter she felt crawling up her throat. Realizing she wasn't going to succeed, she quickly turned her face from Etta and headed toward the door. "Just bring your blasphemin' self on downstairs. I done already missed morning services waiting on you today."

Canaan Baptist Church, a brooding, ashen giant, sat in the middle of a block of rundown private homes. Its multi-colored, dome-shaped eyes glowered into the darkness. Fierce clapping and thunderous organ chords came barreling out of its mouth. Evening services had begun.

Canaan's congregation, the poor who lived in a thirty-block area around Brewster Place, still worshiped God loudly. They could not afford the refined, muted benediction of the more prosperous blacks who went to Sinai Baptist on the northern end of the city, and because each of their requests for comfort was so pressing, they took no chances that He did not hear them.

> When Israel was in Egypt's land
> Let my people go
> Oppressed so hard, they could not stand
> Let my people go

The words were as ancient as the origin of their misery, but the tempo had picked up threefold in its evolution from the cotton fields. They were now sung with the frantic determination of a people who realized that the world was swiftly changing but for some mystic, complex reason their burden had not.

> God said to go down
> Go down
> Brother Moses
> Brother Moses
> To the shore of the great Nile River

The choir clapped and stomped each syllable into a devastating reality, and just as it did, the congregation reached up, grabbed the phrase, and tried to clap and stomp it back into oblivion.

> Go to Egypt
> Go to Egypt
> Tell Pharaoh
> Tell Pharaoh
> Let my people go

Etta entered the back of the church like a reluctant prodigal, prepared at best to be amused. The alien pounding and the heat and the dark glistening bodies dragged her back, back past the cold ashes of her innocence to a time when pain could be castrated on the sharp edges of iron-studded faith. The blood rushed to her temples and began to throb in unison with the musical pleas around her.

> Yes, my God is a mighty God
> Lord, deliver
> And he set old Israel free
> Swallowed that Egyptian army
> Lord, deliver
> With the waves of the great Red Sea

Etta glanced at Mattie, who was swaying and humming, and she saw that the lines in her face had almost totally vanished. She had left Etta in just that moment for a place where she was free. Sadly, Etta looked at her, at them all, and was very envious. Unaccustomed to the irritating texture of doubt, she felt tears as its abrasiveness grated over the fragile skin of her life. Could there have been another way?

The song ended with a huge expulsion of air, and the congregation sat down as one body.

"Come on, let's get us a seat." Mattie tugged her by the arm.

The grizzled church deacon with his suit hanging loosely off his stooped shoulders went up to the pulpit to read the church business.

"That's one of the widowers I was telling you about," Mattie whispered, and poked Etta.

"Unmm." The pressure on her arm brought Etta back onto the uncomfortable wooden pew. But she didn't want to stay there, so she climbed back out the window, through the glass eyes of the seven-foot Good Shepherd, and started again the futile weaving of invisible ifs and slippery mights into an equally unattainable past.

The scenes of her life reeled out before her with the same aging script; but now hindsight sat as the omniscient director and had the young star of her epic recite different brilliant lines and make the sort of stunning decisions that propelled her into the cushioned front pews on the right of the minister's podium. There she sat with the deacons' wives, officers of the Ladies' Auxiliary, and head usherettes. And like them, she would wear on her back a hundred pairs of respectful eyes earned the hard way, and not the way she had earned the red sundress, which she now self-consciously tugged up in the front. Was it too late?

The official business completed, the treasurer pulled at his frayed lapels, cleared his throat, and announced the guest speaker for the night.

The man was magnificent.

He glided to the podium with the effortlessness of a well-oiled machine and stood still for an interminable long moment. He eyed the congregation confidently. He only needed their attention for that split second because once he got it, he was going to wrap his voice around their souls and squeeze until they screamed to be relieved. They knew it was coming and waited expectantly, breathing in unison as one body. First he played with them and threw out fine silken threads that stroked their heart muscles ever so gently. They trembled ecstatically at the touch and invited more. The threads multiplied and entwined themselves solidly around the one pulsating organ they had become and tightened slightly, testing them for a reaction.

The "Amen, brothers" and "Yes, Jesus" were his permission to take that short hop from the heart to the soul and lay all pretense of gentleness aside. Now he would have to push and pound with clenched fists in order to be felt, and he dared not stop the fierce rhythm of his voice until their replies had reached that fevered pitch of satisfaction. Yes, Lord—grind out the unheated tenements! Merciful Jesus— shove aside the low-paying boss man. Perfect Father—fill me, fill me till there's no room, no room for nothing else, not even that great big world out there that exacts such a strange penalty for my being born black.

It was hard work. There was so much in them that had to be replaced. The minister's chest was heaving in long spasms, and the sweat was pouring down his gray temples and rolling under his chin. His rich voice was now hoarse, and his legs and raised arms trembled on the edge of collapse. And as always they were satisfied a half-breath before he reached the end of his endurance. They sat back, limp and spent, but momentarily at peace. There was no price too high for this service. At that instant they would have followed him to do battle with the emperor of the world, and all he was going to ask of them was money for the "Lord's work." And they would willingly give over half of their little to keep this man in comfort.

Etta had not been listening to the message; she was watching the man. His body moved with the air of one who had not known recent deprivation. The tone of his skin and the fullness around his jawline told her that he was well-off, even before she got close enough to see the manicured hands and diamond pinkie ring.

The techniques he had used to brand himself on the minds of the congregation were not new to her. She'd encountered talent like that in poolrooms, nightclubs, grimy second-floor insurance offices, numbers dens, and on a dozen street corners. But here was a different sort of power. The jungle-sharpened instincts of a man like that could move her up to the front of the church, ahead of the deacons' wives and Ladies' Auxiliary, off of Brewster Place for good. She would find not only luxury but a place that complemented the type of woman she had fought all these years to become.

"Mattie, is that your regular minister?" she whispered.

"Who, Reverend Woods? No, he just visits on occasion, but he sure can preach, can't he?"

"What you know about him, he married?"

Mattie cut her eyes at Etta. "I should have figured it wasn't the sermon that moved you. At least wait till after the prayer before you jump all into the man's business."

During the closing song and prayer Etta was planning how she was going to maneuver Mattie to the front of the church and into introducing her to Reverend Woods. It wasn't going to be as difficult as she thought. Moreland T. Woods had noticed Etta from the moment she'd entered the church. She stood out like a bright red bird among the drab morality that dried up the breasts and formed rolls around the stomachs of the other church sisters. This woman was still dripping with the juices of a full-fleshed life—the kind of life he was soon to get up and damn into hell for the rest of the congregation—but how it fitted her well. He had to swallow to remove the excess fluid from his mouth before he got up to preach.

Now the problem was to make his way to the back of the church before she left without seeming to be in a particular hurry. A half-dozen back slaps, handshakes, and thank-you sisters only found him about ten feet up the aisle, and he was growing impatient. However, he didn't dare to turn his neck and look in the direction where he'd last seen her. He felt a hand on his upper arm and turned to see a grim-faced Mattie flanked by the woman in the scarlet dress.

"Reverend Woods, I really enjoyed your sermon," Mattie said.

"Why, thank you, sister—sister?"

"Sister Michael, Mattie Michael." While he was addressing his words to her, the smile he sent over her shoulder to Etta was undeniable.

"Especially the part," Mattie raised her voice a little, "About throwing away temptation to preserve the soul. That was a mighty fine point."

"The Lord moves me and I speak, Sister Michael. I'm just a humble instrument for his voice."

The direction and intent of his smile was not lost to Etta. She inched her way in front of Mattie. "I enjoyed it, too, Reverend Woods. It's been a long time since I heard preaching like that." She increased the pressure of her fingers on Mattie's arm.

"Oh, excuse my manners. Reverend Woods, this is an old friend of mine, Etta Mae Johnson. Etta Mae, Reverend Woods." She intoned the words as if she were reciting a eulogy.

"Please to meet you, Sister Johnson." He beamed down on the small woman and purposely held her hand a fraction longer than usual. "You must be a new member—I don't recall seeing you the times I've been here before."

"Well, no, Reverend, I'm not a member of the congregation, but I was raised up in the church. You know how it is, as you get older sometimes you stray away. But after your sermon, I'm truly thinking of coming back."

Mattie tensed, hoping that the lightning that God was surely going to strike Etta with wouldn't hit her by mistake.

"Well, you know what the Bible says, sister. The angels rejoice more over one sinner who turns around than over ninety-nine righteous ones."

"Yes, indeed, and I'm sure a shepherd like you has helped to turn many back to the fold." She looked up and gave him the full benefit of her round dark eyes, grateful she hadn't put on that third coat of mascara.

"I try, Sister Johnson, I try."

"It's a shame Mrs. Woods wasn't here tonight to hear you. I'm sure she must be mighty proud of your work."

"My wife has gone to her glory, Sister Johnson. I think of myself now as a man alone—rest her soul."

"Yes, rest her soul," Etta sighed.

"Please, Lord, yes," Mattie muttered, giving out the only sincere request among the three. The intensity of her appeal startled them, and they turned to look at her. "Only knows how hard this life is, she's better in the arms of Jesus."

"Yes"—Etta narrowed her eyes at Mattie and then turned back to the minister—"I can testify to that. Being a woman alone, it seems all the more hard. Sometimes you don't know where to turn."

Moreland Woods knew Etta was the type of woman who not only knew which way to turn, but, more often than not, had built her own roads when nothing else was accessible. But he was enjoying this game immensely—almost as much as the growing heat creeping into his groin.

"Well, if I can be of any assistance, Sister Johnson, don't

hesitate to ask. I couldn't sleep knowing one of the Lord's sheep is troubled. As a matter of fact, if you have anything you would like to discuss with me this evening, I'd be glad to escort you home."

"I don't have my own place. You see, I'm just up from out of state and staying with my friend Mattie here."

"Well, perhaps we could all go out for coffee."

"Thank you, but I'll have to decline, Reverend," Mattie volunteered before Etta did it for her. "The services have me all tired out, but if Etta wants to, she's welcome."

"That'll be just fine," Etta said.

"Good, good." And now it was his turn to give her the benefit of a mouth full of strong gold-capped teeth. "Just let me say good-bye to a few folks here, and I'll meet you outside."

"Girl, you oughta patent that speed and sell it to the airplane companies," Mattie said outside. " 'After that sermon, Reverend, I'm thinking of coming back'—indeed!"

"Aw, hush your fussing."

"I declare if you had batted them lashes just a little faster, we'd of had a dust storm in there."

"You said you wanted me to meet some nice men. Well, I met one."

"Etta, I meant a man who'd be serious about settling down with you." Mattie was exasperated. "Why, you're going on like a schoolgirl. Can't you see what he's got in mind?"

Etta turned an indignant face toward Mattie. "The only thing I see is that you're telling me I'm not good enough for a man like that. Oh, no, not Etta Johnson. No upstanding decent man could ever see anything in her but a quick good time. Well, I'll tell you something, Mattie Michael. I've always traveled first class, maybe not in the way you'd approve with all your fine Christian principles, but it's done all right by me. And I'm gonna keep going top drawer till I leave this earth. Don't you think I got a mirror? Each year there's a new line to cover. I lay down with this body and get up with it every morning, and each morning it cries for just a little more rest than it did the day before. Well, I'm finally gonna get that rest, and it's going to be with a man like Reverend Woods. And you and the rest of those slack-mouthed gossips on Brewster be damned!" Tears frosted the edges of her last words. "They'll be humming a different tune when I show up there the wife of a big preacher. I've always known what they say about me behind my back, but I never thought you were right in there with them."

Mattie was stunned by Etta's tirade. How could Etta have so totally misunderstood her words? What had happened back there to stuff up her senses to the point that she had missed the obvious? Surely she could not believe that the vibrations coming from that unholy game of charades in the church aisle would lead to something as permanent as marriage? Why, it had been nothing but the opening gestures to a mating dance. Mattie had gone through the same motions at least once in her life, and Etta must have known a dozen variations to it that were a mystery to her. And yet, somehow, back there it had been played to a music that had totally distorted the steps for her friend. Mattie suddenly felt the helplessness of a person who is forced to explain that for which there are no words.

She quietly turned her back and started down the steps. There was no need to defend herself against Etta's accusations. They shared at least a hundred memories that could belie those cruel words. Let them speak for her.

Sometimes being a friend means mastering the art of timing. There is a time for silence. A time to let go and allow people to hurl themselves into their own destiny. And a time to prepare to pick up the pieces when it's all over. Mattie realized that this moment called for all three.

"I'll see ya when you get home, Etta," she threw gently over her shoulder.

Etta watched the bulky figure become slowly enveloped by the shadows. Her angry words had formed a thick mucus in her throat, and she couldn't swallow them down. She started to run into the darkness where she'd seen Mattie disappear, but at that instant Moreland Woods came out of the lighted church, beaming.

He took her arm and helped her into the front seat of his car. Her back sank into the deep upholstered leather, and the smell of the freshly vacuumed carpet was mellow in her nostrils. All of the natural night sounds of the city were blocked by the thick tinted windows and the hum of the air conditioner, but they trailed persistently behind the polished back of the vehicle as it turned and headed down the long gray boulevard.

> Smooth road
> Clear day
> But why am I the only one
> Traveling this way
> How strange the road to love
> Can be so easy
> Can there be a detour ahead?

Moreland Woods was captivated by the beautiful woman at his side. Her firm brown flesh and bright eyes carried the essence of nectar from some untamed exotic flower, and the fragrance was causing a pleasant disturbance at the pit of his stomach. He marveled at how excellently she played the game. A less alert observer might have been taken in, but his survival depended upon knowing people, knowing exactly how much to give and how little to take. It was this razor-thin instinct that had catapulted him to the head of his profession and that would keep him there.

And although she cut her cards with a reckless confidence, pushed her chips into the middle of the table as though the supply was unlimited, and could sit out the game until dawn, he knew. Oh, yes. Let her win a few, and then he would win just a few more, and she would be bankrupt long before the sun was up. And then there would be only one thing left to place on the table—and she would, because the stakes they were playing for were very high. But she was going to lose that last deal. She would lose because when she first sat down in that car she had everything riding on the fact that he didn't know the game existed.

And so it went. All evening Etta had been in another world, weaving his tailored suit and the smell of his expensive cologne into a custom-made future for herself. It took his last floundering thrusts into her body to bring her back to reality. She arrived in enough time to feel him beating against her like a dying walrus, until he shuddered and was still.

She kept her eyes closed because she knew when she opened them there would be the old familiar sights around her. To her right would be the plastic-coated nightstand that matched the cheaply carved headboard of the bed she lay in. She felt the bleached coarseness of the sheet under her sweaty back and predicted the roughness of the worn carpet path that led from the bed to the white-tiled bathroom with bright fluorescent lights, sterilized towels, and tissue-wrapped water glasses. There would be two or three small thin rectangles of soap wrapped in bright waxy covers that bore the name of the hotel.

She didn't try to visualize what the name would be. It didn't matter. They were all the same, all meshed together into one lump that rested like an iron ball on her chest. And the expression on the face of this breathing mass to her left would be the same as all the others. She could turn now and go through the rituals that would tie up the evening for them both, but she wanted just one more second of this soothing darkness before she had to face the echoes of the locking doors she knew would be in his eyes.

Etta got out of the car unassisted and didn't bother to turn and watch the taillights as it pulled off down the deserted avenue adjacent to Brewster Place. She had asked him to leave her at the corner because there was no point in his having to make a U-turn in the dead-end street, and it was

less than a hundred yards to her door. Moreland was relieved that she had made it easy for him, because it had
been a long day and he was anxious to get home and go to
sleep. But then, the whole business had gone pretty smoothly
after they left the hotel. He hadn't even been called upon to
use any of the excuses he had prepared for why it would be
a while before he'd see her again. A slight frown crossed his
forehead as he realized that she had seemed as eager to get
away from him as he had been to leave. Well, he shrugged
his shoulders and placated his dented ego, that's the nice
part about these wordly women. They understand the tem-
porary weakness of the flesh and don't make it out to be
something bigger than it is. They can have a good time without pawing and hanging all onto a man. Maybe I should drop
around sometime. He glanced into his rearview mirror and
saw that Etta was still standing on the corner, looking straight
ahead into Brewster. There was something about the slumped
profile of her body, silhouetted against the dim street light,
that caused him to press down on the accelerator.

Etta stood looking at the wall that closed off Brewster from
the avenues farther north and found it hard to believe that
it had been just this afternoon when she had seen it. It had
looked so different then, with the August sun highlighting
the browns and reds of the bricks and the young children
bouncing their rubber balls against its side. Now it crouched
there in the thin predawn light, like a pulsating mouth
awaiting her arrival. She shook her head sharply to rid herself of the illusion, but an uncanny fear gripped her, and her
legs felt like lead. If I walk into this street, she thought, I'll
never come back. I'll never get out. Oh, dear God, I am so
tired—so very tired.

Etta removed her hat and massaged her tight forehead.
Then, giving a resigned sigh, she started slowly down the
street. Had her neighbors been out on their front stoops, she
could have passed through their milling clusters as anony-
mously as the night wind. They had seen her come down
that street once in a broken Chevy that had about five

hundred dollars' worth of contraband liquor in its trunk, and there was even the time she'd come home with a broken nose she'd gotten in some hair-raising escapade in St. Louis, but never had she walked among them with a broken spirit. This middle-aged woman in the wrinkled dress and wilted straw hat would have been a stranger to them.

When Etta got to the stoop, she noticed there was a light under the shade at Mattie's window, and she strained to hear what actually sounded like music coming from behind the screen. Mattie was playing her records! Etta stood very still, trying to decipher the broken air waves into intelligible sound, but she couldn't make out the words. She stopped straining when it suddenly came to her that it wasn't important what song it was—someone was waiting up for her. Someone who would deny fiercely that there had been any concern—just a little indigestion from them fried onions that kept me from sleeping. Thought I'd pass the time by figuring out what you see in all this loose-life music.

Etta laughed softly to herself as she climbed the steps toward the light and the love and the comfort that awaited her.

KISWANA
BROWNE

From the window of her sixth-floor studio apartment, Kiswana could see over the wall at the end of the street to the busy avenue that lay just north of Brewster Place. The late-afternoon shoppers looked like brightly clad marionettes as they moved between the congested traffic, clutching their packages against their bodies to guard them from sudden bursts of the cold autumn wind. A portly mailman had abandoned his cart and was bumping into indignant window-shoppers as he puffed behind the cap that the wind had snatched from his head. Kiswana leaned over to see if he was going to be successful, but the edge of the building cut him off from her view.

A pigeon swept across her window, and she marveled at its liquid movements in the air waves. She placed her dreams on the back of the bird and fantasized that it would glide forever in transparent silver circles until it ascended to the center of the universe and was swallowed up. But the wind died down, and she watched with a sigh as the bird beat its wings in awkward, frantic movements to land on the corroded top of a fire escape on the opposite building. This brought her back to earth.

Humph, it's probably sitting over there crapping on those folks' fire escape, she thought. Now, that's a safety hazard. . . . And her mind was busy again, creating flames and smoke and frustrated tenants whose escape was being hindered because they were slipping and sliding in pigeon shit. She watched their cussing, haphazard descent on the fire escapes until they had all reached the bottom. They were milling around, oblivious to their burning apartments, angrily planning to march on the mayor's office about the pigeons. She materialized placards and banners for them, and they had just reached the corner, boldly sidestepping fire hoses and broken glass, when they all vanished.

A tall copper-skinned woman had met this phantom parade at the corner, and they had dissolved in front of her long, confident strides. She plowed through the remains of their faded mists, unconscious of the lingering wisps of their presence on her leather bag and black fur-trimmed coat. It took a few seconds for this transfer from one realm to another to reach Kiswana, but then suddenly she recognized the woman.

"Oh, God, it's Mama!" She looked down guiltily at the forgotten newspaper in her lap and hurriedly circled random job advertisements.

By this time Mrs. Browne had reached the front of Kiswana's building and was checking the house number against a piece of paper in her hand. Before she went into the building she stood at the bottom of the stoop and carefully inspected the condition of the street and the adjoining property. Kiswana watched this meticulous inventory with growing annoyance but she involunarily followed her mother's slowly rotating head, forcing herself to see her new neighborhood through the older woman's eyes. The brightness of the unclouded sky seemed to join forces with her mother as it highlighted every broken stoop railing and missing brick. The afternoon sun glittered and cascaded across even the tiniest fragments of broken bottle, and at that very moment the wind chose to rise up again, sending unswept grime flying into the air, as a stray tin can left by careless garbage collectors went rolling noisily down the center of the street.

Kiswana noticed with relief that at least Ben wasn't sitting in his usual place on the old garbage can pushed against the far wall. He was just a harmless old wino, but Kiswana knew her mother only needed one wino or one teenager with a reefer within a twenty-block radius to decide that her daughter was living in a building seething with dope factories and hang-outs for derelicts. If she had seen Ben, nothing would have made her believe that practically every apartment contained a family, a Bible, and a dream that one day enough could be scraped from those meager Friday night paychecks to make Brewster Place a distant memory.

As she watched her mother's head disappear into the building, Kiswana gave silent thanks that the elevator was broken. That would give her at least five minutes' grace to straighten up the apartment. She rushed to the sofa bed and hastily closed it without smoothing the rumpled sheets and blanket or removing her nightgown. She felt that somehow the tangled bedcovers would give away the fact that she had not slept alone last night. She silently apologized to Abshu's memory as she heartlessly crushed his spirit between the steel springs of the couch. Lord, that man was sweet. Her toes curled involuntarily at the passing thought of his full lips moving slowly over her instep. Abshu was a foot man, and he always started his lovemaking from the bottom up. For that reason Kiswana changed the color of the polish on her toenails every week. During the course of their relationship she had gone from shades of red to brown and was now into the purples. I'm gonna have to start mixing them soon, she thought aloud as she turned from the couch and raced into the bathroom to remove any traces of Abshu from there. She took up his shaving cream and razor and threw them into the bottom drawer of her dresser beside her diaphragm. Mama wouldn't dare pry into my drawers right in front of me, she thought as she slammed the drawer shut. Well, at least not the *bottom* drawer. She may come up with some sham excuse for opening the top drawer, but never the bottom one.

When she heard the first two short raps on the door, her eyes took a final flight over the small apartment, desperately seeking out any slight misdemeanor that might have to be defended. Well, there was nothing she could do about the crack in the wall over that table. She had been after the landlord to fix it for two months now. And there had been no time to sweep the rug, and everyone knew that off-gray always looked dirtier than it really was. And it was just too damn bad about the kitchen. How was she expected to be out job-hunting every day and still have time to keep a kitched that looked like her mother's, who didn't even work and still had someone come in twice a month for general cleaning. And besides . . .

Her imaginary argument was abruptly interrupted by a second series of knocks, accompanied by a penetrating, "Melanie, Melanie, are you there?"

Kiswana strode toward the door. She's starting before she even gets in here. She knows that's not my name anymore.

She swung the door open to face her slightly flushed mother. "Oh, hi, Mama. You know, I thought I heard a knock, but I figured it was for the people next door, since no one hardly ever calls me Melanie." Score one for me, she thought.

"Well, it's awfully strange you can forget a name you answered to for twenty-three years," Mrs. Browne said, as she moved past Kiswana into the apartment. "My, that was a long climb. How long has your elevator been out? Honey, how do you manage with your laundry and groceries up all those steps? But I guess you're young, and it wouldn't bother you as much as it does me." This long string of questions told Kiswana that her mother had no intentions of beginning her visit with another argument about her new African name.

"You know I would have called before I came, but you don't have a phone yet. I didn't want you to feel that I was snooping. As a matter of fact, I didn't expect to find you home at all. I thought you'd be out looking for a job." Mrs. Browne had mentally covered the entire apartment while she was talking and taking off her coat.

"Well, I got up late this morning. I thought I'd buy the afternoon paper and start early tomorrow."

"That sounds like a good idea." Her mother moved toward the window and picked up the discarded paper and glanced over the hurriedly circled ads. "Since when do you have experience as a fork-lift operator?"

Kiswana caught her breath and silently cursed herself for her stupidity. "Oh, my hand slipped—I meant to circle file clerk." She quickly took the paper before her mother could see that she had also marked cutlery salesman and chauffeur.

"You're sure you weren't sitting here moping and daydreaming again?" Amber specks of laughter flashed in the corner of Mrs. Browne's eyes.

Kiswana threw her shoulders back and unsuccessfully tried to disguise her embarrassment with indignation.

"Oh, God, Mama! I haven't done that in years—it's for kids. When are you going to realize that I'm a woman now?" She sought desperately for some womanly thing to do and settled for throwing herself on the couch and crossing her legs in what she hoped looked like a nonchalant arc.

"Please, have a seat," she said, attempting the same tones and gestures she'd seen Bette Davis use on the late movies.

Mrs. Browne, lowering her eyes to hide her amusement, accepted the invitation and sat at the window, also crossing her legs. Kiswana saw immediately how it should have been done. Her celluloid poise clashed loudly against her mother's quiet dignity, and she quickly uncrossed her legs. Mrs. Browne turned her head toward the window and pretended not to notice.

"At least you have a halfway decent view from here. I was wondering what lay beyond that dreadful wall—it's the boulevard. Honey, did you know that you can see the trees in Linden Hills from here?"

Kiswana knew that very well, because there were many lonely days that she would sit in her gray apartment and stare at those trees and think of home, but she would rather have choked than admit that to her mother.

"Oh, really, I never noticed. So how is Daddy and things at home?"

"Just fine. We're thinking of redoing one of the extra bedrooms since you children have moved out, but Wilson insists that he can manage all that work alone. I told him that he doesn't really have the proper time or energy for all that. As it is, when he gets home from the office, he's so tired he can hardly move. But you know you can't tell your father anything. Whenever he starts complaining about how stubborn you are, I tell him the child came by it honestly. Oh, and your brother was by yesterday," she added, as if it had just occurred to her.

So that's it, thought Kiswana. That's why she's here.

Kiswana's brother, Wilson, had been to visit her two days ago, and she had borrowed twenty dollars from him to get her winter coat out of layaway. That son-of-a-bitch probably ran straight to Mama—and after he swore he wouldn't say anything. I should have known, he was always a snotty-nosed sneak, she thought.

"Was he?" she said aloud. "He came by to see me, too, earlier this week. And I borrowed some money from him because my unemployment checks hadn't cleared in the bank, but now they have and everything's just fine." There, I'll beat you to that one.

"Oh, I didn't know that," Mrs. Browne lied. "He never mentioned you. He had just heard that Beverly was expecting again, and he rushed over to tell us."

Damn. Kiswana could have strangled herself.

"So she's knocked up again, huh?" she said irritably.

Her mother started. "Why do you always have to be so crude?"

"Personally, I don't see how she can sleep with Willie. He's such a dishrag."

Kiswana still resented the stance her brother had taken in college. When everyone at school was discovering their blackness and protesting on campus, Wilson never took part; he had even refused to wear an Afro. This had outraged Kiswana because, unlike her, he was dark-skinned and had the type of hair that was thick and kinky enough for a good "Fro." Kiswana had still insisted on cutting her own hair, but it was so thin and fine-textured, it refused to thicken even after she washed it. So she had to brush it up and spray it with lacquer to keep it from lying flat. She never forgave Wilson for telling her that she didn't look African, she looked like an electrocuted chicken.

"Now that's some way to talk. I don't know why you have an attitude against your brother. He never gave me a restless night's sleep, and now he's settled with a family and a good job."

"He's an assistant to an assistant junior partner in a law firm. What's the big deal about that?"

"The job has a future, Melanie. And at least he finished school and went on for his law degree."

"In other words, not like me, huh?"

"Don't put words into my mouth, young lady. I'm perfectly capable of saying what I mean."

Amen, thought Kiswana.

"And I don't know why you've been trying to start up with me from the moment I walked in. I didn't come here to fight with you. This is your first place away from home, and I just wanted to see how you were living and if you're doing all right. And I must say, you've fixed this apartment up very nicely."

"Really, Mama?" She found herself softening in the light of her mother's approval.

"Well, considering what you had to work with." This time she scanned the apartment openly.

"Look, I know it's not Linden Hills, but a lot can be done with it. As soon as they come and paint, I'm going to hang my Ashanti print over the couch. And I thought a big Boston Fern would go well in that corner, what do you think?"

"That would be fine, baby. You always had a good eye for balance."

Kiswana was beginning to relax. There was little she did that attracted her mother's approval. It was like a rare bird, and she had to tread carefully around it lest it fly away.

"Are you going to leave that statue out like that?"

"Why, what's wrong with it? Would it look better some-where else?"

There was a small wooden reproduction of a Yoruba god-dess with large protruding breasts on the coffee table.

"Well," Mrs. Browne was beginning to blush, "it's just that it's a bit suggestive, don't you think? Since you live alone now, and I know you'll be having male friends stop by, you wouldn't want to be giving them any ideas. I mean, uh, you know, there's no point in putting yourself in any unpleasant situations because they may get the wrong impressions and uh, you know, I mean, well . . ." Mrs. Browne stammered on miserably.

Kiswana loved it when her mother tried to talk about sex. It was the only time she was at a loss for words.

"Don't worry, Mama." Kiswana smiled. "That wouldn't bother the type of men I date. Now maybe if it had big feet . . ." And she got hysterical, thinking of Abshu.

Her mother looked at her sharply. "What sort of gibberish is that about feet? I'm being serious, Melanie."

"I'm sorry, Mama." She sobered up. "I'll put it away in the closet," she said, knowing that she wouldn't.

"Good," Mrs. Browne said, knowing that she wouldn't either. "I guess you think I'm too picky, but we worry about you over here. And you refuse to put in a phone so we can call and see about you."

"I haven't refused, Mama. They want seventy-five dollars for a deposit, and I can't swing that right now."

"Melanie, I can give you the money."

"I don't want you to be giving me money—I've told you that before. Please, let me make it by myself."

"Well, let me lend it to you, then."

"No!"

"Oh, so you can borrow money from your brother, but not from me."

Kiswana turned her head from the hurt in her mother's

eyes. "Mama, when I borrow from Willie, he makes me pay him back. You never let me pay you back," she said into her hands.

"I don't care. I still think it's downright selfish of you to be sitting over here with no phone, and sometimes we don't hear from you in two weeks—anything could happen— especially living among these people."

Kiswana snapped her head up. "What do you mean, *these people*. They're my people and yours, too, Mama—we're all black. But maybe you've forgotten that over in Linden Hills."

"That's not what I'm talking about, and you know it. These streets—this building—it's so shabby and rundown. Honey, you don't have to live like this."

"Well, this is how poor people live."

"Melanie, you're not poor."

"No, Mama, *you're* not poor. And what you have and I have are two totally different things. I don't have a husband in real estate with a five-figure income and a home in Linden Hills—*you* do. What I have is a weekly unemployment check and an overdrawn checking account at United Federal. So this studio on Brewster is all I can afford."

"Well, you could afford a lot better," Mrs. Browne snapped, "if you hadn't dropped out of college and had to resort to these dead-end clerical jobs."

"Uh-huh, I knew you'd get around to that before long." Kiswana could feel the rings of anger begin to tighten around her lower backbone, and they sent her forward onto the couch. "You'll never understand, will you? Those bourgie schools were counterrevolutionary. My place was in the streets with my people, fighting for equality and a better community."

"Counterrevolutionary!" Mrs. Browne was raising her voice. "Where's your revolution now, Melanie? Where are all those black revolutionaries who were shouting and demonstrating and kicking up a lot of dust with you on that campus? Huh? They're sitting in wood-paneled offices with their degrees in mahogany frames, and they won't even drive their cars past this street because the city doesn't fix potholes in this part of town."

"Mama," she said, shaking her head slowly in disbelief, "how can you—a black woman—sit there and tell me that what we fought for during the Movement wasn't important just because some people sold out?"

"Melanie, I'm not saying it wasn't important. It was damned important to stand up and say that you were proud of what you were and to get the vote and other social opportunities for every person in this country who had it due. But you kids thought you were going to turn the world upside down, and it just wasn't so. When all the smoke had cleared, you found yourself with a fistful of new federal laws and a country still full of obstacles for black people to fight their way over—just because they're black. There was no revolution, Melanie, and there will be no revolution."

"So what am I supposed to do, huh? Just throw up my hands and not care about what happens to my people? I'm not supposed to keep fighting to make things better?"

"Of course, you can. But you're going to have to fight within the system, because it and these so-called 'bourgie' schools are going to be here for a long time. And that means that you get smart like a lot of your old friends and get an important job where you can have some influence. You don't have to sell out, as you say, and work for some corporation, but you could become an assemblywoman or a civil liberties lawyer or open a freedom school in this very neighborhood. That way you could really help the community. But what help are you going to be to these people on Brewster while you're living hand-to-mouth on file-clerk jobs waiting for a revolution? You're wasting your talents, child."

"Well, I don't think they're being wasted. At least I'm here in day-to-day contact with the problems of my people. What good would I be after four or five years of a lot of white brainwashing in some phony, prestige institution, huh? I'd be like you and Daddy and those other educated blacks sitting over there in Linden Hills with a terminal case of middle-class amnesia."

"You don't have to live in a slum to be concerned about social conditions, Melanie. Your father and I have been charter members of the NAACP for the last twenty-five years."

"Oh, God!" Kiswana threw her head back in exaggerated disgust. "That's being concerned? That middle-of-the-road, Uncle Tom dumping ground for black Republicans!"

"You can sneer all you want, young lady, but that organization has been working for black people since the turn of the century, and it's still working for them. Where are all those radical groups of yours that were going to put a Cadillac in every garage and Dick Gregory in the White House? I'll tell you where."

I knew you would, Kiswana thought angrily.

"They burned themselves out because they wanted too much too fast. Their goals weren't grounded in reality. And that's always been your problem."

"What do you mean, my problem? I know exactly what I'm about."

"No, you don't. You constantly live in a fantasy world—always going to extremes—turning butterflies into eagles, and life isn't about that. It's accepting what is and working from that. Lord, I remember how worried you had me, putting all that lacquered hair spray on your head. I thought you were going to get lung cancer—trying to be what you're not."

Kiswana jumped up from the couch. "Oh, God, I can't take this anymore. Trying to be something I'm not—trying to be something I'm not, Mama! Trying to be proud of my heritage and the fact that I was of African descent. If that's being what I'm not, then I say fine. But I'd rather be dead than be like you—a white man's nigger who's ashamed of being black!"

Kiswana saw streaks of gold and ebony light follow her mother's flying body out of the chair. She was swung around by the shoulders and made to face the deadly stillness in the angry woman's eyes. She was too stunned to cry out from the pain of the long fingernails that dug into her shoulders, and she was brought so close to her mother's face that she saw her reflection, distorted and wavering, in the tears that stood in the older woman's eyes. And she listened in that stillness to a story she had heard from a child.

"My grandmother," Mrs. Browne began slowly in a whisper, "was a full-bloodied Iroquois, and my grandfather a free black from a long line of journeymen who had lived in Connecticut since the establishment of the colonies. And my father was a Bajan who came to this country as a cabin boy on a merchant mariner."

"I know all that," Kiswana said, trying to keep her lips from trembling.

"Then, know this." And the nails dug deeper into her flesh. "I am alive because of the blood of proud people who never scraped or begged or apologized for what they were. They lived asking only one thing of this world—to be allowed to be. And I learned through the blood of these people that black isn't beautiful and it isn't ugly—black is! It's not kinky hair and it's not straight hair—it just is.

"It broke my heart when you changed your name. I gave you my grandmother's name, a woman who bore nine children and educated them all, who held off six white men with a shotgun when they tried to drag one of her sons to jail for 'not knowing his place.' Yet you needed to reach into an African dictionary to find a name to make you proud.

"When I brought my babies home from the hospital, my ebony son and my golden daughter, I swore before whatever gods would listen—those of my mother's people or those of my father's people—that I would use everything I had and could ever get to see that my children were prepared to meet this world on its own terms, so that no one could sell them short and make them ashamed of what they were or how they looked—whatever they were or however they looked. And Melanie, that's not being white or red or black—that's being a mother."

Kiswana followed her reflection in the two single tears that
moved down her mother's cheeks until it blended with them
into the woman's copper skin. There was nothing and then
so much that she wanted to say, but her throat kept closing
up every time she tried to speak. She kept her head down
and her eyes closed, and thought, Oh, God, just let me die.
How can I face her now?

Mrs. Browne lifted Kiswana's chin gently. "And the one
lesson I wanted you to learn is not to be afraid to face anyone, not even a crafty old lady like me who can outtalk you."
And she smiled and winked.

"Oh, Mama, I . . ." and she hugged the woman tightly.

"Yeah, baby." Mrs. Browne patted her back. "I know."
She kissed Kiswana on the forehead and cleared her throat.
"Well, now, I better be moving on. It's getting late, there's
dinner to be made, and I have to get off my feet—these new
shoes are killing me."

Kiswana looked down at the beige leather pumps. "Those
are really classy. They're English, aren't they?"

"Yes, but, Lord, do they cut me right across the instep."
She removed the shoe and sat on the couch to massage her
foot.

Bright red nail polish glared at Kiswana through the stockings. "Since when do you polish your toenails?" she gasped.
"You never did that before."

"Well . . ." Mrs. Browne shrugged her shoulders, "your
father sort of talked me into it, and, uh, you know, he likes it
and all, so I thought, uh, you know, why not, so . . ." And
she gave Kiswana an embarrassed smile.

I'll be damned, the young woman thought, feeling her
whole face tingle. Daddy's into feet! And she looked at the
blushing woman on her couch and suddenly realized that her
mother had trod through the same universe that she herself
was now traveling. Kiswana was breaking no new trails
and would eventually end up just two feet away on that
couch. She stared at the woman she had been and was to
become.

"But I'll never be a Republican," she caught herself saying aloud.

"What are you mumbling about, Melanie?" Mrs. Browne slipped on her shoe and got up from the couch.

She went to get her mother's coat. "Nothing, Mama. It's really nice of you to come by. You should do it more often."

"Well, since it's not Sunday, I guess you're allowed at least one lie."

They both laughed.

After Kiswana had closed the door and turned around, she spotted an envelope sticking between the cushions of her couch. She went over and opened it up; there was seventy-five dollars in it.

"Oh, Mama, darn it!" She rushed to the window and started to call to the woman, who had just emerged from the building, but she suddenly changed her mind and sat down in the chair with a long sigh that caught in the upward draft of the autumn wind and disappeared over the top of the building.

LUCIELIA LOUISE TURNER

The sunlight was still watery as Ben trudged into Brewster Place, and the street had just begun to yawn and stretch itself. He eased himself onto his garbage can, which was pushed against the sagging brick wall that turned Brewster into a dead-end street. The metallic cold of the can's lid seeped into the bottom of his thin trousers. Sucking on a piece of breakfast sausage caught in his back teeth, he began to muse. Mighty cold, these spring mornings. The old days you could build a good trash fire in one of them barrels to keep warm. Well, don't want no summons now, and can't freeze to death. Yup, can't freeze to death.

His daily soliloquy completed, he reached into his coat pocket and pulled out a crumpled brown bag that contained his morning sun. The cheap red liquid moved slowly down his throat, providing immediate justification as the blood began to warm in his body. In the hazy light a lean dark figure began to make its way slowly up the block. It hesitated in front of the stoop at 316, but looking around and seeing Ben, it hurried over.

"Yo, Ben."

"Hey, Eugene, I thought that was you. Ain't seen ya round for a coupla days."

"Yeah." The young man put his hands in his pockets, frowned into the ground, and kicked the edge of Ben's can. "The funeral's today, ya know."

"Yeah."

"You going?" He looked up into Ben's face.

"Naw, I ain't got no clothes for them things. Can't abide 'em no way—too sad—it being a baby and all."

"Yeah. I was going myself, people expect it, ya know?"

"Yeah."

"But, man, the way Ciel's friends look at me and all—like I was filth or something. Hey, I even tried to go see Ciel in the hospital, heard she was freaked out and all."

"Yeah, she took it real bad."

"Yeah, well, damn, I took it bad. It was my kid, too, ya know. But Mattie, that fat, black bitch, just standin' in the hospital hall sayin' to me—to me, now, 'Whatcha want?' Like I was a fuckin' germ or something. Man, I just turned and left. You gotta be treated with respect, ya know?"

"Yeah."

"I mean, I should be there today with my woman in the limo and all, sittin' up there, doin' it right. But how you gonna be a man with them ball-busters tellin' everybody it was my fault and I should be the one dead? Damn!"

"Yeah, a man's gotta be a man." Ben felt the need to wet his reply with another sip. "Have some?"

"Naw, I'm gonna be heading on—Ciel don't need me today. I bet that frig, Mattie, rides in the head limo, wearing the pants. Shit—let 'em." He looked up again. "Ya know?"

"Yup."

"Take it easy, Ben." He turned to go.

"You too, Eugene."

"Hey, you going?"

"Naw."

"Me neither. Later."

"Later, Eugene."

Funny, Ben thought, Eugene ain't stopped to chat like that for a long time—near on a year, yup, a good year. He took another swallow to help him bring back the year-old conversation, but it didn't work; the second and third one didn't either. But he did remember that it had been an early spring morning like this one, and Eugene had been wearing those same tight jeans. He had hestitated outside of 316 then, too. But that time he went in . . .

Lucielia had just run water into the tea kettle and was putting it on the burner when she heard the cylinder turn. He didn't have to knock on the door; his key still fit the lock. Her thin knuckles gripped the handle of the kettle, but she didn't turn around. She knew. The last eleven months of her life hung compressed in the air between the click of the lock and his "Yo, baby."

The vibrations from those words rode like parasites on the air waves and came rushing into her kitchen, smashing the compression into indistinguishable days and hours that swirled dizzily before her. It was all there: the frustration of being left alone, sick, with a month-old baby; her humiliation reflected in the caseworker's blue eyes for the unanswerable "you can find him to have it, but can't find him to take care of it" smile; the raw urges that crept, uninvited, between her thighs on countless nights; the eternal whys all meshed with the explainable hate and unexplainable love. They kept circling in such a confusing pattern before her that she couldn't seem to grab even one to answer him with. So there was nothing in Lucielia's face when she turned it toward Eugene, standing in her kitchen door holding a ridiculously pink Easter bunny, nothing but sheer relief. . . .

"So he's back." Mattie sat at Lucielia's kitchen table, playing with Serena. It was rare that Mattie ever spoke more than two sentences to anybody about anything. She didn't have to. She chose her words with the grinding precision of a diamond cutter's drill.

"You think I'm a fool, don't you?"

"I ain't said that."

"You didn't have to," Ciel snapped.

"Why you mad at me, Ciel? It's your life, honey."

"Oh, Mattie, you don't understand. He's really straightened up this time. He's got a new job on the docks that pays real good, and he was just so depressed before with the new baby and no work. You'll see. He's even gone out now to buy paint and stuff to fix up the apartment. And, and Serena needs a daddy."

"You ain't gotta convince me, Ciel."

No, she wasn't talking to Mattie, she was talking to herself. She was convincing herself it was the new job and the paint and Serena that let him back into her life. Yet, the real truth went beyond her scope of understanding. When she laid her head in the hollow of his neck there was a deep musky scent to his body that brought back the ghosts of the Tennessee soil of her childhood. It reached up and lined the inside of her nostrils so that she inhaled his presence almost every minute of her life. The feel of his sooty flesh penetrated the skin of her fingers and coursed through her blood and became one, somewhere, wherever it was, with her actual being. But how do you tell yourself, let alone this practical old woman who loves you, that he was back because of that. So you don't.

You get up and fix you both another cup of coffee, calm the fretting baby on your lap with her pacifier, and you pray silently—very silently—behind veiled eyes that the man will stay.

Ciel was trying to remember exactly when it had started to go wrong again. Her mind sought for the slender threads of a clue that she could trace back to—perhaps—something she had said or done. Her brow was set tightly in concentration as she folded towels and smoothed the wrinkles over and over, as if the answer lay concealed in the stubborn creases of the terry cloth.

The months since Eugene's return began to tick off slowly before her, and she examined each one to pinpoint when the nagging whispers of trouble had begun in her brain. The friction on the towels increased when she came to the month that she had gotten pregnant again, but it couldn't be that. Things were different now. She wasn't sick as she had been with Serena, he was still working—no it wasn't the baby. It's not the baby, it's not the baby—the rhythm of those words sped up the motion of her hands, and she had almost yanked and folded and pressed them into a reality when, bewildered, she realized that she had run out of towels.

Ciel jumped when the front door slammed shut. She waited tensely for the metallic bang of his keys on the coffee table and the blast of the stereo. Lately that was how Eugene announced his presence home. Ciel walked into the living room with the motion of a swimmer entering a cold lake.

"Eugene, you're home early, huh?"

"You see anybody else sittin' here?" He spoke without looking at her and rose to turn up the stereo.

He wants to pick a fight, she thought, confused and hurt. He knows Serena's taking her nap, and now I'm supposed to say, Eugene, the baby's asleep, please cut the music down. Then he's going to say, you mean a man can't even relax in his own home without being picked on? I'm not picking on you, but you're going to wake up the baby. Which is always supposed to lead to: You don't give a damn about me. Everybody's more important than me—that kid, your friends, everybody. I'm just chickenshit around here, huh?

All this went through Ciel's head as she watched him leave the stereo and drop defiantly back down on the couch. Without saying a word, she turned and went into the bedroom. She looked down on the peaceful face of her daughter and softly caressed her small cheek. Her heart became full as she realized, this is the only thing I have ever loved without pain. She pulled the sheet gently over the tiny shoulders and firmly closed the door, protecting her from the music. She then went into the kitchen and began washing the rice for their dinner.

Eugene, seeing that he had been left alone, turned off the stereo and came and stood in the kitchen door.

"I lost my job today," he shot at her, as if she had been the cause.

The water was turning cloudy in the rice pot, and the force of the stream from the faucet caused scummy bubbles to rise to the surface. These broke and sprayed tiny starchy particles onto the dirty surface. Each bubble that broke seemed to increase the volume of the dogged whispers she had been ignoring for the last few months. She poured the dirty water off the rice to destroy and silence them, then watched with a malicious joy as they disappeared down the drain.

"So now, how in the hell I'm gonna make it with no money, huh? And another brat comin' here, huh?"

The second change of the water was slightly clearer, but the starch-speckled bubbles were still there, and this time there was no way to pretend deafness to their message. She had stood at that sink countless times before, washing rice, and she knew the water was never going to be totally clear. She couldn't stand there forever—her fingers were getting cold, and the rest of the dinner had to be fixed, and Serena would be waking up soon and wanting attention. Feverishly she poured the water off and tried again.

"I'm fuckin' sick of never getting ahead. Babies and bills, that's all you good for."

The bubbles were almost transparent now, but when they broke they left light trails of starch on top of the water that curled around her fingers. She knew it would be useless to try again. Defeated, Ciel placed the wet pot on the burner, and the flames leaped up bright red and orange, turning the water droplets clinging on the outside into steam.

Turning to him, she silently acquiesced. "All right, Eugene, what do you want me to do?"

He wasn't going to let her off so easily. "Hey, baby, look, I don't care what you do. I just can't have all these hassles on me right now, ya know?"

"I'll get a job. I don't mind, but I've got no one to keep Serena, and you don't want Mattie watching her."

"Mattie—no way. That fat bitch'll turn the kid against me.

She hates my ass, and you know it."

"No, she doesn't, Eugene." Ciel remembered throwing that at Mattie once. "You hate him, don't you?" "Naw, honey," and she had cupped both hands on Ciel's face. "Maybe I just loves you too much."

"I don't give a damn what you say—she ain't minding my kid."

"Well, look, after the baby comes, they can tie my tubes— I don't care." She swallowed hard to keep down the lie.

"And what the hell we gonna feed it when it gets here, huh—air? With two kids and you on my back, I ain't never gonna have nothin'." He came and grabbed her by the shoulders and was shouting into her face. "Nothin', do you hear me, nothin'!"

"Nothing to it, Mrs. Turner." The face over hers was as calm and antiseptic as the room she lay in. "Please, relax. I'm going to give you a local anesthetic and then perform a simple D&C, or what you'd call a scraping to clean out the uterus. Then you'll rest here for about an hour and be on your way. There won't even be much bleeding." The voice droned on in its practiced monologue, peppered with sterile kindness.

Ciel was not listening. It was important that she keep herself completely isolated from these surroundings. All the activities of the past week of her life were balled up and jammed on the right side of her brain, as if belonging to some other woman. And when she had endured this one last thing for her, she would push it up there, too, and then one day give it all to her—Ciel wanted no part of it.

The next few days Ciel found it difficult to connect herself up again with her own world. Everything seemed to have taken on new textures and colors. When she washed the dishes, the plates felt peculiar in her hands, and she was more conscious of their smoothness and the heat of the water. There was a disturbing split second between someone talking to her and the words penetrating sufficiently to elicit a response. Her neighbors left her presence with slight frowns of puzzlement, and Eugene could be heard mumbling, "Moody bitch."

She became terribly possessive of Serena. She refused to leave her alone, even with Eugene. The little girl went everywhere with Ciel, toddling along on plump uncertain legs. When someone asked to hold or play with her, Ciel sat nearby, watching every move. She found herself walking into the bedroom several times when the child napped to see if she was still breathing. Each time she chided herself for this unreasonable foolishness, but within the next few minutes some strange force still drove her back.

Spring was slowly beginning to announce itself at Brewster Place. The arthritic cold was seeping out of the worn gray bricks, and the tenants with apartment windows facing the street were awakened by six o'clock sunlight. The music no longer blasted inside of 3C, and Ciel grew strong with the peacefulness of her household. The playful laughter of her daughter, heard more often now, brought a sort of redemption with it.

"Isn't she marvelous, Mattie? You know she's even trying to make whole sentences. Come on, baby, talk for Auntie Mattie."

Serena, totally uninterested in living up to her mother's proud claims, was trying to tear a gold-toned button off the bosom of Mattie's dress.

"It's so cute. She even knows her father's name. She says, my da da is Gene."

"Better teach her your name," Mattie said, while playing with the baby's hand. "She'll be using it more."

Ciel's mouth flew open to ask her what she meant by that, but she checked herself. It was useless to argue with Mattie. You could take her words however you wanted. The burden of their truth lay with you, not her.

Eugene came through the front door and stopped short when he saw Mattie. He avoided being around her as much as possible. She was always polite to him, but he sensed a silent condemnation behind even her most innocent words. He constantly felt the need to prove himself in front of her. These frustrations often took the form of unwarranted rudeness on his part.

Serena struggled out of Mattie's lap and went toward her father and tugged on his legs to be picked up. Ignoring the child and cutting short the greetings of the two women, he said coldly, "Ciel, I wanna talk to you."

Sensing trouble, Mattie rose to go. "Ciel, why don't you let me take Serena downstairs for a while. I got some ice cream for her."

"She can stay right here," Eugene broke in. "If she needs ice cream, I can buy it for her."

Hastening to soften his abruptness, Ciel said, "That's okay, Mattie, it's almost time for her nap. I'll bring her later—after dinner."

"All right. Now you all keep good." Her voice was warm. "You too, Eugene," she called back from the front door.

The click of the lock restored his balance to him. "Why in the hell is she always up here?"

"You just had your chance—why didn't you ask her yourself? If you don't want her here, tell her to stay out," Ciel snapped back confidently, knowing he never would.

"Look, I ain't got time to argue with you about that old hag. I got big doings in the making, and I need you to help me pack." Without waiting for a response, he hurried into the bedroom and pulled his old leather suitcase from under the bed.

A tight, icy knot formed in the center of Ciel's stomach and began to melt rapidly, watering the blood in her legs so that they almost refused to support her weight. She pulled Serena back from following Eugene and sat her in the middle of the living room floor.

"Here, honey, play with the blocks for Mommy—she has

to talk to Daddy." She piled a few plastic alphabet blocks in front of the child, and on her way out of the room, she glanced around quickly and removed the glass ashtrays off the coffee table and put them on a shelf over the stereo.

Then, taking a deep breath to calm her racing heart, she started toward the bedroom.

Serena loved the light colorful cubes and would some-times sit for an entire half-hour, repeatedly stacking them up and kicking them over with her feet. The hollow sound of their falling fascinated her, and she would often bang two of them together to re-create the magical noise. She was sit-ting, contentedly engaged in this particular activity, when a slow dark movement along the baseboard caught her eye.

A round black roach was making its way from behind the couch toward the kitchen. Serena threw one of her blocks at the insect, and, feeling the vibrations of the wall above it, the roach sped around the door into the kitchen. Finding a totally new game to amuse herself, Serena took off behind the insect with a block in each hand. Seeing her moving toy trying to bury itself under the linoleum by the garbage pail she threw another block, and the frantic roach now raced along the wall and found security in the electric wall socket under the kitchen table.

Angry at losing her plaything, she banged the block against the socket, attempting to get it to come back out. When that failed, she unsuccessfully tried to poke her chubby finger into the thin horizontal slit. Frustrated, tiring of the game, she sat under the table and realized she had found an en-tirely new place in the house to play. The shiny chrome of the table and chair legs drew her attention, and she experi-mented with the sound of the block against their smooth sur-faces.

This would have entertained her until Ciel came, but the roach, thinking itself safe, ventured outside of the socket.

Serena gave a cry of delight and attempted to catch her lost playmate, but it was too quick and darted back into the wall. She tried once again to poke her finger into the slit. Then a bright slender object, lying dropped and forgotten, came into her view. Picking up the fork, Serena finally managed to fit the thin flattened prongs into the electric socket.

Eugene was avoiding Ciel's eyes as he packed. "You know, baby, this is really a good deal after me bein' out of work for so long." He moved around her still figure to open the drawer that held his T-shirts and shorts. "And hell, Maine ain't far. Once I get settled on the docks up there, I'll be able to come home all the time."

"Why can't you take us with you?" She followed each of his movements with her eyes and saw herself being buried in the case under the growing pile of clothes.

" 'Cause I gotta check out what's happening before I drag you and the kid up there."

"I don't mind. We'll make do. I've learned to live on very little."

"No, it just won't work right now. I gotta see my way clear first."

"Eugene, please." She listened with growing horror to herself quietly begging.

"No, and that's it!" He flung his shoes into the suitcase.

"Well, how far is it? Where did you say you were going?" She moved toward the suitcase.

"I told ya—the docks in Newport."

"That's not in Maine. You said you were going to Maine."

"Well, I made a mistake."

"How could you know about a place so far up? Who got you the job?"

"A friend."

"Who?"

"None of your damned business!" His eyes were flashing

with the anger of a caged animal. He slammed down the top of the suitcase and yanked it off the bed.

"You're lying, aren't you? You don't have a job, do you? Do you?"

"Look, Ciel, believe whatever the fuck you want to. I gotta go." He tried to push past her.

She grabbed the handle of the case. "No, you can't go."

"Why?"

Her eyes widened slowly. She realized that to answer that would require that she uncurl that week of her life, pushed safely up into her head, when she had done all those terrible things for that other woman who had wanted an abortion. She and she alone would have to take responsibility for them now. He must understand what those actions had meant to her, but somehow, he had meant even more. She sought desperately for the right words, but it all came out as—

"Because I love you."

"Well, that ain't good enough."

Ciel had let the suitcase go before he jerked it away. She looked at Eugene, and the poison of reality began to spread through her body like gangrene. It drew his scent out of her nostrils and scraped the veil from her eyes, and he stood before her just as he really was—a tall, skinny black man with arrogance and selfishness twisting his mouth into a strange shape. And, she thought, I don't feel anything now. But soon, very soon, I will start to hate you. I promise—I will hate you. And I'll never forgive myself for not having done it sooner—soon enough to have saved my baby. Oh, dear God, my baby.

Eugene thought the tears that began to crowd into her eyes were for him. But she was allowing herself this one last luxury of brief mourning for the loss of something denied to her. It troubled her that she wasn't sure exactly what that something was, or which one of them was to blame for taking it away. Ciel began to feel the overpowering need to be near someone who loved her. I'll get Serena and we'll go visit

Mattie now, she thought in a daze.

Then they heard the scream from the kitchen.

The church was small and dark. The air hung about them like a stale blanket. Ciel looked straight ahead, oblivious to the seats filling up behind her. She didn't feel the damp pressure of Mattie's heavy arm or the doubt that invaded the air over Eugene's absence. The plaintive Merciful Jesuses, lightly sprinkled with sobs, were lost on her ears. Her dry eyes were locked on the tiny pearl-gray casket, flanked with oversized arrangements of red-carnationed bleeding hearts and white-lilied eternal circles. The sagging chords that came loping out of the huge organ and mixed with the droning voice of the black-robed old man behind the coffin were also unable to penetrate her.

Ciel's whole universe existed in the seven feet of space between herself and her child's narrow coffin. There was not even room for this comforting God whose melodious virtues floated around her sphere, attempting to get in. Obviously, He had deserted or damned her, it didn't matter which. All Ciel knew was that her prayers had gone unheeded—that afternoon she had lifted her daughter's body off the kitchen floor, those blank days in the hospital, and now. So she was left to do what God had chosen not to.

People had mistaken it for shock when she refused to cry. They thought it some special sort of grief when she stopped eating and even drinking water unless forced to; her hair went uncombed and her body unbathed. But Ciel was not grieving for Serena. She was simply tired of hurting. And she was forced to slowly give up the life that God had refused to take from her.

After the funeral the well-meaning came to console and offer their dog-eared faith in the form of coconut cakes, potato pies, fried chicken, and tears. Ciel sat in the bed with her back resting against the headboard; her long thin fingers, still as midnight frost on a frozen pond, lay on the covers. She acknowledged their kindnesses with nods of her head and slight lip movements, but no sound. It was as if her voice was too tired to make the journey from the diaphragm through the larynx to the mouth.

Her visitors' impotent words flew against the steel edge of her pain, bled slowly, and returned to die in the senders' throats. No one came too near. They stood around the door and the dressing table, or sat on the edges of the two worn chairs that needed upholstering, but they unconsciously pushed themselves back against the wall as if her hurt was contagious.

A neighbor woman entered in studied certainty and stood in the middle of the room. "Child, I know how you feel, but don't do this to yourself. I lost one, too. The Lord will . . ." And she choked, because the words were jammed down into her throat by the naked force of Ciel's eyes. Ciel had opened them fully now to look at the woman, but raw fires had eaten them worse than lifeless—worse than death. The woman saw in that mute appeal for silence the ragings of a personal hell flowing through Ciel's eyes. And just as she went to reach for the girl's hand, she stopped as if a muscle spasm had overtaken her body and, cowardly, shrank back. Reminiscences of old, dried-over pains were no consolation in the face of this. They had the effect of cold beads of water on a hot iron—they danced and fizzled up while the room stank from their steam.

Mattie stood in the doorway, and an involuntary shudder went through her when she saw Ciel's eyes. Dear God, she thought, she's dying, and right in front of our faces.

"Merciful Father, no!" she bellowed. There was no prayer, no bended knee or sackcloth supplication in those words, but a blasphemous fireball that shot forth and went smashing against the gates of heaven, raging and kicking, demanding to be heard.

"No! No! No!" Like a black Brahman cow, desperate to protect her young, she surged into the room, pushing the neighbor woman and the others out of her way. She approached the bed with her lips clamped shut in such force that the muscles in her jaw and the back of her neck began to ache.

She sat on the edge of the bed and enfolded the tissue-thin body in her huge ebony arms. And she rocked. Ciel's body was so hot it burned Mattie when she first touched her, but she held on and rocked. Back and forth, back and forth—she had Ciel so tightly she could feel her young breasts flatten against the buttons of her dress. The black mammoth gripped so firmly that the slightest increase of pressure would have cracked the girl's spine. But she rocked.

And somewhere from the bowels of her being came a moan from Ciel, so high at first it couldn't be heard by anyone there, but the yard dogs began an unholy howling. And Mattie rocked. And then, agonizingly slow, it broke its way through the parched lips in a spaghetti-thin column of air that could be faintly heard in the frozen room.

Ciel moaned. Mattie rocked. Propelled by the sound, Mattie rocked her out of that bed, out of that room, into a blue vastness just underneath the sun and above time. She rocked her over Aegean seas so clean they shone like crystal, so clear the fresh blood of sacrificed babies torn from their mother's arms and given to Neptune could be seen like pink froth on the water. She rocked her on and on, past Dachau, where soul-gutted Jewish mothers swept their children's entrails off laboratory floors. They flew past the spilled brains of Senegalese infants whose mothers had dashed them on the wooden sides of slave ships. And she rocked on.

She rocked her into her childhood and let her see murdered dreams. And she rocked her back, back into the womb, to the nadir of her hurt, and they found it—a slight silver splinter, embedded just below the surface of the skin. And Mattie rocked and pulled—and the splinter gave way, but its roots were deep, gigantic, ragged, and they tore up flesh with bits of fat and muscle tissue clinging to them. They left a huge hole, which was already starting to pus over, but Mattie was satisfied. It would heal.

The bile that had formed a tight knot in Ciel's stomach began to rise and gagged her just as it passed her throat. Mattie put her hand over the girl's mouth and rushed her out the now-empty room to the toilet. Ciel retched yellowish-green phlegm, and she brought up white lumps of slime that hit the seat of the toilet and rolled off, splattering onto the tiles. After a while she heaved only air, but the body did not seem to want to stop. It was exorcising the evilness of pain.

Mattie cupped her hands under the faucet and motioned for Ciel to drink and clean her mouth. When the water left Ciel's mouth, it tasted as if she had been rinsing with a mild acid. Mattie drew a tub of hot water and undressed Ciel. She let the nightgown fall off the narrow shoulders, over the pitifully thin breasts and jutting hipbones. She slowly helped her into the water, and it was like a dried brown autumn leaf hitting the surface of a puddle.

And slowly she bathed her. She took the soap, and, using only her hands, she washed Ciel's hair and the back of her neck. She raised her arms and cleaned the armpits, soaping well the downy brown hair there. She let the soap slip between the girl's breasts, and she washed each one separately, cupping it in her hands. She took each leg and even cleaned under the toenails. Making Ciel rise and kneel in the tub, she cleaned the crack in her behind, soaped her pubic hair, and gently washed the creases in her vagina— slowly, reverently, as if handling a newborn.

She took her from the tub and toweled her in the same manner she had been bathed—as if too much friction would break the skin tissue. All of this had been done without either woman saying a word. Ciel stood there, naked, and felt the cool air play against the clean surface of her skin. She had the sensation of fresh mint coursing through her pores. She closed her eyes and the fire was gone. Her tears no longer fried within her, killing her internal organs with their steam. So Ciel began to cry—there, naked, in the center of the bathroom floor. — Vulnerable.

Mattie emptied the tub and rinsed it. She led the still-naked Ciel to a chair in the bedroom. The tears were flowing so freely now Ciel couldn't see, and she allowed herself to be led as if blind. She sat on the chair and cried—head erect. Since she made no effort to wipe them away, the tears dripped down her chin and landed on her chest and rolled down to her stomach and onto her dark pubic hair. Ignoring Ciel, Mattie took away the crumpled linen and made the bed, stretching the sheets tight and fresh. She beat the pillows into a virgin plumpness and dressed them in white cases.

And Ciel sat. And cried. The unmolested tears had rolled down her parted thighs and were beginning to wet the chair. But they were cold and good. She put out her tongue and began to drink in their saltiness, feeding on them. The first tears were gone. Her thin shoulders began to quiver, and spasms circled her body as new tears came—this time, hot and stinging. And she sobbed, the first sound she'd made since the moaning.

Mattie took the edges of the dirty sheet she'd pulled off the bed and wiped the mucus that had been running out of Ciel's nose. She then led her freshly wet, glistening body, baptized now, to the bed. She covered her with one sheet and laid a towel across the pillow—it would help for a while.

And Ciel lay down and cried. But Mattie knew the tears would end. And she would sleep. And morning would come.

CORA LEE

True, I talk of dreams,
Which are the children of an idle brain
Begot of nothing but vain fantasy

Her new baby doll. They placed the soft plastic and pink flannel in the little girl's lap, and she turned her moon-shaped eyes toward them in awed gratitude. It was so perfect and so small. She trailed her fingertips along the smooth brown forehead and down into the bottom curve of the upturned nose. She gently lifted the dimpled arms and legs and then reverently placed them back. Slowly kissing the set painted mouth, she inhaled its new aroma while stroking the silken curled head and full cheeks. She circled her arms around the motionless body and squeezed, while with tightly closed eyes she waited breathlessly for the first trembling vibrations of its low, gravelly "Mama" to radiate through her breast. Her parents surrounded this annual ritual with full heavy laughter, patted the girl on the head, and returned to the other business of Christmas.

Cora Lee was an easy child to please. She asked for only this one thing each year, and although they supplied her over the years with the blocks, bicycles, books, and games they felt necessary for a growing child, she spent all of her time with her dolls—and they had to be baby dolls. She told them this with a silent rebellion the year they had decided she was now old enough for a teenaged Barbie doll; they had even sacrificed for an expensive set of foreign figurines with porcelain faces and real silk and lace mantillas, saris, and kimonos. The following week they found the dolls under her bed with the heads smashed in and the arms twisted out of their sockets.

That was when her father began to worry. Nonsense, her mother had replied. Wasn't he always saying that she was different from their other children? Well, all children were careless with their toys, and this only proved that she was just like the rest. But the woman stared around the room, thoughtfully fingering the broken pieces of china, while her daughter's assortment of diapered and bottled dolls stared back from their neat row with fixed smiles.

They reluctantly bowed in the face of her quiet reproach and soothed their bruised authority by giving her cheaper and cheaper baby dolls. But their laughter grew hollow and disquieting over Cora's Christmas ritual with the plastic and flannel because her body was now growing rounded and curved. Her father quickly averted his face and busied himself with the other children during the moments that her mother would first hand her the doll from under the tree. Yet a lump still formed in his throat from the lingering glimpse of her melted gratitude for the gift of dead plastic.

He put his foot down on her thirteenth Christmas. There would be no more dolls—of any kind. Let her go play like other children her age. But she does play like other children, her mother pleaded. She had secretly watched her daughter over the years for some missing space, some faintly visible sign in her schoolwork or activities that would explain the strange Christmas ritual, but there was none. She wasn't as bright as her brother, but her marks were a great deal better than her sister's, and she was certainly their most obedient child. Was he going to deny her child this one thing that made her happy? He silently turned from the anger that his seeming unreasonableness fixed on his wife's face, because there were no words for the shudder that went through his mind at the memory of the dead brown plastic resting on his daughter's protruding breasts.

In his guilt and bewilderment he spent more money on her that Christmas than on all the other children, but they still felt the quiet reproach in her spirit as she listlessly fingered the new sweaters, camera, and portable radio.

"That's okay, baby," her mother whispered in her ear, "you have lots of dolls in your room."

"But they don't smell and feel the same as the new ones." And the woman was startled by the depths of misery and loss reflected on the girl's dark brown face. She quickly pushed the image away from herself and still refused to believe that there was any need to worry. And it would be many months later before she recalled that image to her consciousness. It would return to her after her youngest daughter would approach her with the news one afternoon that Cora Lee had been doing nasty with the Murphy boy behind the basement steps. And she would call her older daughter to her and hear her recount with a painful innocence that it wasn't nasty, he had just promised to show her the thing that felt good in the dark—and it had felt good, Mother.

And she would then sadly and patiently give an explanation, long overdue, that Cora Lee mustn't let the Murphy boy or any other boy show her the thing that felt good in the dark, because her body could now make babies and she wasn't old enough to be a mother. Did she understand? And as she would watch the disjointed mysteries of life connect up in her daughter's mind and hear her breathe out with enlightened wonder—"A real baby, Mother?"—the image of that Christmas would come smashing into her brain like a meat cleaver. It was then that she began to worry.

"Cora, Cora Lee!" The voice echoed shrilly up the air shaft. "I told ya to stop them goddamned children from jumping over my goddamned head all the goddamned day! Now I'm gonna call the police—do you hear me? The goddamned police!" And the window banged shut.

Cora Lee sighed slowly, turned her head from her soap

opera, and looked around the disheveled living room at the howling and flying bodies that were throwing dingy school books at each other, jumping off of crippled furniture, and swinging on her sagging velveteen draperies.

"Y'all stop that now," she called out languidly. "You're giving Miss Sophie a nervous headache, and she said she's gonna call the cops." No one paid her any attention, and she turned back toward the television with a sigh, absentmindedly stroking the baby on her lap. What did these people on Brewster Place want from her anyway? Always complaining. If she let the kids go outside, they made too much noise in the halls. If they played in the streets, she didn't watch them closely enough. How could she do all that—be a hundred places at one time? It was enough just trying to keep this apartment together. Did she know little Brucie was going to climb the wall at the end of the block and fall and break his arm? The way they had carried on, you'd think she had pushed him off herself.

Bruce ran in front of the television, chasing one of his sisters and trying to hit her over the head with his dirty unraveling cast.

"Stop that, you're messing up the picture," she said irritably. Now the doctors were saying that his arm wasn't mending right and she had to bring him back to have it reset. Always something—she must remember to look at the clinic card for his next appointment. Tuesday the something, she faintly recalled. She hoped it wasn't last Tuesday, or she would have to wait forever for a new appointment.

"I just don't know," she sighed aloud, shifted the baby into her arms, and got up to adjust the picture and change channels. She hated it when her two favorite stories came on at the same time; it was a pain to keep switching channels between Steve's murder trial and Jessica's secret abortion.

A rubber ball came hurling across the room and smacked the baby on the side of the head. It began screaming, and her eyes blazed around the room for the offender.

"All right, that's it!" she yelled, charging around the room, hitting randomly at whoever wasn't quick enough to dodge her swinging fists. "Now just get outside—I'm sick of you. Wait! Doesn't anyone have any homework?" She only threatened them with homework when they had pushed her to the end of her patience. She listened suspiciously to the mottled chorus of "nos" to her question, but couldn't gather the energy to sort through the confused pile of torn notebooks that lay scattered about the floor.

"Awful strange," she muttered darkly. "No one ever has any homework. When I was in school, we always got homework." But they had already headed for the door, knowing she had used up her ultimate weapon against them. "And we didn't get left back like you little dumb asses," she called out impotently to the slamming door. It had surprised her when Maybelline had gotten left back. Her oldest daughter had always liked school, and there were never any truant notices for her in the mailbox like there were for the others. Take her to the library, the teachers had said, encourage her to read. But the younger ones had torn and marked in her library books, and they made you pay for that. She couldn't afford to be paying for books all the time. And how was she expected to keep on top of them every minute? It was enough just trying to keep the apartment together. She underscored that thought by picking up a handful of discarded clothes and throwing them into a leaning chair. So now truant notices were coming for Maybelline, too.

"I just don't know," she sighed, and sat back down in front of the television. She gently examined the side of the baby's head to see if the ball had left a mark and kissed the tiny bruise. Why couldn't they just stay like this—so soft and easy to care for? How she had loved them this way. Taking the baby's hand in her mouth, she sucked at the small fingers and watched it giggle and try to reach for her nose. She poked her thumb into the dimpled cheek and lifted the child onto her breast so she could stroke its finely curled hair and inhale the mingled sweetness of mineral oil and talcum powder that lay in the creases of its neck. Oh, for them to stay like this, when they could be fed from her body so there were no welfare offices to sit in all day or food stamp lines to stand on, when she alone could be their substance and their world, when there were no neighbors or teachers or social workers to answer to about their actions. They stayed where you put them and were so easy to keep clean.

She'd spend hours washing, pressing, and folding the miniature clothes, blankets, and sheets. The left-hand corner of her bedroom which held the white wooden crib and dresser was dusted and mopped religiously. As she got on her hands and knees to wash the molding under the crib, the red and black sign in the clinic glared into her mind—GERMS ARE YOUR BABY'S ENEMIES—and she was constantly alert for any of them hidden in that left-hand corner. No, when her babies slept she made sure they went unmolested by those things painted on that clinic poster. There was no place for them to hide on that brown body that was bathed and oiled twice a day, or in the folds of the pastel flannel and percales that she personally scrubbed and sterilized, or between the bristles of the hair brushes that were boiled each week and replaced each month. She couldn't bear the thought of those ugly red things creeping into the soft, fragrant curls that she now buried her nose into.

She wondered at the change in the fine silky strands that moved with the slightest force of her breath and raised to tickle her nostrils when she inhaled. In a few years they would grow tight and kinky and rough. She'd hate to touch them then, because the child would cry when she yanked the comb through its matted hair. And she would have to drag them from under the bed or out of closets and have to thump them on the head constantly to get them to sit still while she combed their hair. And if she didn't, there would now be neighbors and teachers and a motley assortment of relatives to complain about the linty, gnarled hair of the babies who had grown beyond the world of her lap, growing wild-eyed and dumb, coming home filthy from the streets with rough corduroy, khaki, and denim that tattered faster than she could mend, and with mouthfuls of rotten teeth, and scraped limbs, and torn school books, and those damned truant notices in her mailbox—dumb, just plain dumb.

"Are you gonna be a dumb-ass too?" she cooed at the baby. "No, not Mama's baby. You're not gonna be like them."

There was no reason for them being like that—so difficult. She had gone to school until her sophomore year, when she had her first baby. And in those days you had to leave high school if you were pregnant. She had intended to go back, but the babies just seemed to keep coming—always welcome until they changed, and then she just didn't understand them.

Don't understand you, Cora Lee, just don't understand you. Having all them babies year after year by God knows who. Only Sammy and Maybelline got the same father. Daughter, what's wrong with you? Sis, what's wrong with you? Case number 6348, what's wrong with you?

What was wrong with them? If they behaved better, people wouldn't always be on her back. Maybe Sammy and Maybelline's father would have stayed longer. She had really liked him. His gold-capped teeth and glass eye had fascinated her, and she had almost learned to cope with his peculiar ways. A pot of burnt rice would mean a fractured jaw, or a wet bathroom floor a loose tooth, but that had been their fault for keeping her so tied up she couldn't keep the house straight. But she still carried the scar under her left eye because of a baby's crying, and you couldn't stop a baby from crying. Babies had to cry sometimes, and so Sammy and Maybelline's father had to go. And then there was Brucie's father, who had promised to marry her and take her off Welfare, but who went out for a carton of milk and never came back. And then only the shadows—who came in the night and showed her the thing that felt good in the dark, and often left before the children awakened, which was so much better—there was no more waiting for a carton of milk that never came and no more bruised eyes because of a baby's crying. The thing that felt good in the dark would sometimes bring the new babies, and that's all she cared to know, since the shadows would often lie about their last names or their jobs or about not having wives. She had stopped listening, stopped caring to know. It was too much trouble, and it didn't matter because she had her babies. And shadows didn't give you fractured jaws or bruised eyes, there was no time for all that—in the dark—before the children awakened.

She turned her head toward the door and sighed when she heard the knock. Now what? It couldn't be the kids, once they were out she had to go down and scrape them from the streets unless they got too cold or hungry. Did that cranky old woman really call the cops? She opened the door and faced a tall pretty young girl with beaded hair, holding a struggling and cursing Sammy by the collar and a stack of papers in the other arm. The other children littered the hallway and stairs to watch their brother's ordeal.

"Mama, I ain't done nothing. Tell this shit face; I ain't done nothing."

"What a way to talk." She snatched him and flung him into the apartment. "Missy, I'm sorry. Did he steal something from you? He's always taking things and I've beat him about it but he still won't stop. I've told the little dumb-ass the teachers have threatened to send him to reform school." She turned toward her son. "Do you hear that—*reform school*, you little . . ."

"No, wait, you've got it all wrong—it's not that!" The girl shifted the papers in her arm uncomfortably. "He was downstairs eating out of one of the garbage cans and I thought you oughta know because, well, he might be hungry or something."

"Oh," Cora Lee seemed relieved, "I know he does that." She saw the girl's eyes widen slightly in disbelief. "He's looking for sweets. The dentist at the clinic said all his teeth are rotten so I won't give him anything sweet and he searches through garbage cans for them. I tried to make him stop but you can't be everywhere at once. I figure once he gets sick enough from that filthy habit, he'll stop by himself."

The girl was still staring at her. Cora went on, "Believe me, my kids get plenty to eat. I got two full books of food stamps I haven't used yet. I don't know why I bother to cook; they just mess over their food—always eating that damned candy. But I had to stop Sammy because the doctors said his gums were infected and I didn't want that spreading to the baby." Why was this girl looking at her so strangely? She probably thought she was lying. Sammy was really gonna get it for embarrassing her like this. "I was just about to cook dinner when you came to the door," she lied. She still had two more stories to watch before forcing herself to face the greasy sinkful of day-old dishes and pots that had to be cleared away before making dinner. "Okay, y'all," she called over the girl's shoulder, "come on in the house, it's almost time to eat."

Howls of protest and disbelief followed in the wake of her words and she ran out in the hall behind the retreating footsteps. "I said get your ass in this house!" she yelled. "Or you gonna be damned sorry!" The unaccustomed force in her voice stunned them into a reluctant obedience. They sulked past her into the apartment with a series of sucking teeth and "we never eat this earlys" that were not lost on the girl.

Cora smiled triumphantly at the girl and let out a long sigh. "You see what I mean—they're terrible. I just don't know."

"Yes," the girl looked down uneasily at her papers, "it must be difficult with so many. I'm sorry I had to meet you like this but I was coming by anyway." She looked up and slipped into a practiced monologue. "I'm Kiswana Browne and I live up on the sixth floor. I'm trying to start a tenants' association on this block. You know, all of these buildings are owned by one man and if we really pull together, we can put pressure on him to start fixing this place up. Once we get the association rolling we can even stage a rent strike and do the repairs ourselves. I'd like you to check off on this sheet all the things that are wrong with your apartment and then I'm going to take these forms and file them at the housing court."

Cora Lee listened to Kiswana's musical, clipped accent, looked at the designer jeans and striped silk blouse, and was surprised she had said that she lived in this building. What was she doing on a street like Brewster? She couldn't have been here very long or she would know there was nothing you could do about the way things were. That white man didn't care about what a bunch of black folks had to say, and these people weren't gonna stick together no way. They were too busy running around complaining, trying to make trouble for her instead of the landlord. It's a shame she's wasting her time because she seems like a nice girl.

"There's plenty wrong with this place, but this ain't gonna do no good."

"It will if we can get enough people to sign these forms. I've already been through four of the buildings and the response is really great. We'll be having our first meeting this Saturday at noon."

"I just don't know," Cora sighed and looked around her apartment. Kiswana openly followed her gaze and Cora Lee answered what she saw reflected in the girl's face. "You know, you can't keep nothing nice with these kids tearing up all the time. My sister gave me that living room set only six months ago and it was practically new."

"No, I know what you mean," Kiswana said a little too quickly as her eyes passed over the garbage spilling out of the kitchen can.

"You got kids then?"

"No, but my brother has two and he says they can really be a handful at times."

"Well, I got a lot more than that so you can imagine the hell I go through."

Kiswana jumped as they heard a loud crash and a scream coming from the corner of the room. Cora Lee turned around placidly and without moving called to the child tangled in the fallen curtain rods and drapery. "You happy now, Dorian? Huh? I told ya a million times to stop swinging on my curtains, so good for you!"

Kiswana pushed past her and went toward the screaming child. "Maybe he's hurt his head."

"Naw, he's always falling from something. He's got a head like a rock." Cora followed her to examine her curtains and see if they were torn. "He's just like his father—all those West Indians got hard heads." Well, at least, I guess he was West Indian, she thought, he had some kind of accent. "This curtain rod's totally gone." She glared down at the child Kiswana was cradling. "And I got no more money to replace it, so these drapes can just stay down for all I care."

Dorian had stopped crying and was feeling the colorful beads attached to Kiswana's braids.

"Leave her hair alone and get up and go in the other room."

Kiswana looked up at Cora alarmed. "There's a big knot coming up on the side of his head; maybe we should take him . . ."

"It'll go down," Cora said and went to the couch and picked up the baby. Kiswana was still holding Dorian and made no attempt to hide the disapproval on her face. "Look," Cora Lee said, "if I ran to the hospital every time one of these kids bumps their head or scrapes their knee, I'd spend the rest of my life in those emergency rooms. You just don't know—they're wild and disgusting and there's nothing you can do!" She rocked the baby energetically as if the motions of her body could build up a wall against the girl's silent condemnation.

Dorian tried to snatch one of the beads twisted in Kiswana's hair and she cried out in pain as he jumped from her lap with the end of a braid clenched in his fist. "Son-of-a . . . !" flew out of her mouth before she stopped herself and bit on her lip.

"See what I mean?" Cora almost smiled gratefully at Dorian as he raced around the door into the other room.

"You know," Kiswana got off her knees and brushed the dust from her jeans, "they're probably that way from being cramped up in this apartment all the time. Kids need space to move around in."

"There's plenty of room in that school yard for them to play, but will they go to school? No. And the last time I let them go to the park somebody gave Sammy a reefer and when my mother found it in his pocket, I caught hell for that. So what am I supposed to do? I gotta keep them away from there or I'll end up with a bunch of junkies on my hands."

She saw out of the corner of her eye that *Another World* was going off. Aw shit! Now she wouldn't know until Monday if Rachel had divorced Mack because he'd become impotent after getting caught in that earthquake. Why didn't this girl just go home and stop minding her business.

"Look, I have your paper and I'll look it over, okay? But I got a million things to do right now so you can come back for it some other time." She knew she was being rude, but there were only three commercials left before *The Doctors* started.

"Oh, sure, I'm sorry; I didn't mean to keep you. You know, I wasn't trying to tell you how to raise your children or anything. It's just that . . ." She involuntarily glanced around the living room again.

"Yeah, I know," Cora said with one eye on the television, "it's just that I'm busy right now. You see, I got to get up . . ."

"And cook dinner," Kiswana said sadly.

"Yeah, right—dinner." And she went to open the door.

Kiswana seemed reluctant to move. "You know, there's a lot of good things that go on in the park too." She pulled a leaflet out of her pocketbook. "My boyfriend's gotten a grant from the city and he's putting on a black production of *A Midsummer Night's Dream* this weekend. Maybe you could come and bring the children," she offered, barely hopeful.

Cora looked begrudgingly at the flyer. "Abshu Ben-Jamal Productions," she mouthed slowly. "Hey, I know him—a big, dark fellow. Didn't he have a traveling puppet show last summer?"

"Yes, that's him." Kiswana smiled.

"Came around here with a truck or something and little dancing African dolls. I remember; the kids talked about it for weeks."

"You see," Kiswana hurried on encouraged, "they love things like that. Why don't you bring them tomorrow night?"

"I don't know," Cora sighed and looked at the leaflet. "This stuff here—Shakespeare and all that. It'll be too deep for them and they'll start acting up and embarrassing me in front of all those people."

"Oh, no—they'll love it," Kiswana insisted. "It's going to be funny and colorful and he's brought it up to date. There's music and dancing—he's going to have the actors do the Hustle around a maypole—and they slap each other five and all sorts of stuff like that. And it'll have fairies—all kids like stories with fairies and things in them; even if they don't understand every word, it'll be great for them. Please, try to come."

"Well, I'll see. Saturday is pretty busy for me. I have to clean up the baby's things and do the wash. Then there's so many of them to get ready. I don't know; I'll try."

"Look, I'm not doing much tomorrow. After the tenants' meeting, I'll come by early and help you with the kids. Then we can all go together. Okay? It'll be fun."

Aw dammit! She could hear the opening music to *The Doctors*. Anything to get rid of this girl. "Okay, I'll bring them, but you don't have to stop by. I'll manage alone; I'm used to it."

"No, I want to. It's no problem."

"Yeah, but they'll just show off if you're here. It'll be easier if I get them ready myself." She swung the door open.

"Okay, then I'll wait and stop by for you on my way out.

How about six-thirty so we can get good seats?"

"Yeah, all right—six-thirty." And she opened the door a little wider.

Kiswana was elated and she cooed at the baby, "Hear that, sweetie? You're going to a play." She stroked the child under the chin. "She's a fine little thing. What's her name?"

Her attentions to the baby bought her a few more minutes of Cora Lee's time. "Sonya Marie," she said and proudly hoisted the child up to be admired.

"She looks just like you." Kiswana took the baby and tickled her nose with the end of one of her braids.

"It's a shame you ain't got none of your own. You're good with kids."

"I don't have a husband, yet," Kiswana answered automatically, watching the baby laugh.

"So, neither do I." Cora shrugged her shoulders.

Kiswana looked up and added quickly, "Well, someday, maybe, but right now all I have is a studio."

"Babies don't take up much space. You just bring in a crib and a little chest and you're all set," Cora beamed.

"But babies grow up," Kiswana said softly and handed the child back to Cora with a puzzled smile.

Cora Lee shut the door and sat back down in front of the television, but Maggie's battle with the rare blood disease she'd contracted in Guatemala flickered by unnoticed. There was no longer any comfort in stroking the child on her lap. Kiswana's perfume, lingering in the air mixed with the odor of stale food and old dust, left her unsettled and she couldn't pinpoint exactly why. After a few restless moments, she laid the baby on the couch and went over to the stack of albums she kept on a corner table. She slowly flipped through the expensive studio poses of her babies. Dorian, Brucie, Sammy, Maybelline—Dierdre and Daphane (how pleased she had been that year to have two come at once). Her babies—all her babies—stared back at her, petrified under the yellowing plastic. She must get Sonya's pictures taken before it was too late.

But babies grow up

She looked at the hanging draperies, the broken furniture, the piles of litter in her living room. That girl probably thought that she was a bad mother. But she loved her babies! Her babies—her . . . She began to go through the albums again—Shakespeare, humph. Her class had gone to see Shakespeare when she was in junior high. She stared into Maybelline's brown, infant eyes—*We are such stuff as dreams are made on, and our little life is rounded with a sleep*—Where had that come from? Had the teacher made them memorize that from the play, "The Temple," or something it was called. She had loved school; she always went to school—not like them. Why didn't her babies go to school? She shook her head confusedly. No, babies didn't go to school. Sonya was her baby and she was too little for school. Sonya was never any trouble. Sonya. . .

But babies grow up

She slammed the album shut. That girl probably thought she didn't want to take her children to that play. Why shouldn't they go? It would be good for them. They needed things like Shakespeare and all that. They would do better in school and stop being so bad. They'd grow up to be like her sister and brother. Her brother had a good job in the post office and her sister lived in Linden Hills. She should have told that girl that—her sister was married to a man with his own business and a big house in Linden Hills. That would have shown her—coming in here with her fancy jeans and silk blouse, saying she was a bad mother. Yeah, she'd have her babies ready tomorrow.

Cora Lee went and turned off the television and decided to start dinner early after all.

"Why we gotta take a bath—Grandma's coming over?"
"No, you're going to a play." Cora Lee was changing the

water in the tub for the third shift of children.

"I don't wanna go to no play," Dorian protested.

"Yes, you do," she said, stripping him and throwing him into the sudsy water. "And if you know what's good for you, you'll stay in that tub." She went through the door to find Brucie.

"Dierdre, you can't wear those socks—they got holes in them."

"But I always wear these to school."

"Well, you're not wearing them like that tonight—give 'em to me!" She took the socks from the girl, dragged Brucie into the tub, and went in search of a needle and thread.

The children followed her bewildering behavior with freshly combed and brushed heads. They had never seen their mother so active. The feeling had begun after breakfast when she took their plates from the table, washed and stacked them, and swept the kitchen floor before moving into the living room to leave it dusted and in some semblance of order, and then on to the bedrooms, where she had even changed their sheets—there was something in the air. It felt like Christmas or a visit from their grandparents, but neither of these was happening, so they exchanged troubled glances and moved cautiously about with only token protests to the stranger who had awakened them that morning.

Cora sorted feverishly through their clothes—washing, pressing, and mending. She couldn't believe they were in such a state. Trouser legs were ankle-high or frayed to distraction, dresses were ripped from the waist and unraveled at the hem, socks were missing entire toes or heels—when had all this happened? She patched and fussed, meshed and mated outfits until she was finally satisfied with the neatly buttoned bodies she assembled before her. She lined up the scoured faces, carefully parted hair, and oiled arms and legs on the couch, and forbid them to move.

When she opened the door for Kiswana, the girl was touched as she sensed the amount of effort that must have gone into the array of roughly patched trousers, ill-fitting shirts, and unevenly hemmed dresses that the woman proudly presented to her. She smiled warmly into Cora Lee's eyes. "Well, I see we're all set. Let's go." She took the two smallest hands in hers and they all trooped down the steps.

Cora flanked the group like a successful drill sergeant, and she made a point of personally addressing each neighbor that was standing on the stoop and along the outside railing, ignoring the openly surprised stares as they emerged from the building. Where could she be going with all them kids? The welfare office wasn't open. She was greeted with the friendly caution that women hold toward unmarried women who repeatedly have children—since they aren't having them by their own husbands, there is always the possibility they are having them by yours.

Mattie was coming up the block, wheeling a heavy shopping cart.

"Hi, Miss Mattie," Cora called out warmly. She sincerely liked Mattie because unlike the others, Mattie never found the time to do jury duty on other people's lives.

"Why, hello y'all. My don't we look nice. Where you going?"

"To the park—for Shakespeare." Cora emphasized the last word, extending her smile into a semicircle that covered the other listening ears.

"That's right nice. This the new baby? Ain't she pretty. You gonna have to stop this soon, Cora. You got a full load now," Mattie chided lightly.

"I know, Miss Mattie," Cora sighed. "But how you gonna stop?"

"Same way you started, child—only in reverse." The three women laughed.

"Sammy, help Miss Mattie up the steps with that cart and then meet us at the end of the alley." They were approaching the six-foot alley that lay between Mattie's building and the wall on Brewster Place.

"Naw, I can manage. I don't want him walking in that alley alone; it's getting dark. C. C. Baker and all them lowlifes be hanging around there, smoking that dope. I done called the police on 'em a hundred times, but they won't come for that."

Mattie and Kiswana spoke a few minutes about the new tenants' association getting the city to fence off the alley, and then the group moved on. They approached the park and then followed the huge red arrows painted under the green and black letters—A Midsummer Night's Dream—toward the center. Cora had come to the park prepared. She had a leather strap folded up in her bag and she placed herself in the middle of the row with the children seated on both sides of her so no one would be beyond the reach of her arm. Kiswana sat on the end, holding Sonya. They weren't going to cut up and embarrass her in front of these people. They would sit still and get this Shakespeare thing if she had to break their backs.

She looked around and didn't recognize anyone from Brewster so the blacks here probably came from Linden Hills, and over half of the people filtering in were white. This must really be something if they were coming. She straightened up on the rough bench, poked Brucie and Dorian, who were sitting on either side of her, and threw invisible threats to the left and right at the others. There would be no fidgeting and jumping up—show these people that they were used to things like this. She uncurled Bruce's collar and motioned to Daphane to close her legs and pull down her dress.

The evening light had turned into the color of faded navy blue blankets when the spotlights came on. Cora couldn't understand what the actors were saying, but she had never heard black people use such fine-sounding words, and they really seemed to know what they were talking about—no one was forgetting the lines or anything. She looked to see if she would have to sneak her strap out of her bag, but the children were surprisingly still, except for Dorian, and she only had to jab him twice because when they changed the set for the forest scenes, even he was awed. That girl was right—it was simply beautiful. Huge papier-mâché flora hung in varying shades of green splendor among sequin-dusted branches and rocks. The fairy people were dressed in gold and lavender gauze with satin trimming that glimmered under the colored spotlight. And the Lucite crowns worn on stage split the floodlights into a multitude of dancing, elongated diamonds.

At first Cora took her cues from the people around her and laughed when they did, but as the play gained momentum the evident slapstick quality in the situation drew its own humor. The fairy man had done something to the eyes of these people and everyone seemed to be chasing everyone else. First, that girl in brown liked that man and Cora laughed naturally as he hit and kicked her to keep her from following him because he was after the girl in white who was in love with someone else again. But after the fairy man messed with their eyes, the whole thing turned upside down and no one knew what was going on—not even the people in the play.

That fairy queen looked just like Maybelline. Maybelline could be doing this some day—standing on a stage, wearing pretty clothes, and saying fine things. That girl had probably gone to college for that. But Maybelline could go to college—she liked school.

"Mama," Brucie whispered, "am I gonna look like that? Is that what a dumb-ass looks like when it grows up?"

The character, Bottom, was prancing on the stage, wearing an ass's head.

Cora felt the guilt lining her mouth seep down to form a lump in her throat. "No, baby." She stroked his head. "Mama won't let you look like that."

"But isn't that man a dumb-ass, too? Don't they look . . ."

"Shhh, we'll talk about it later."

The next scene was blurred in front of her. Maybelline used to like school—why had she stopped? The image of the torn library books and unanswered truant notices replaced the tears in her eyes as they quietly rolled down her face.

School would be over in a few weeks, but all this truant nonsense had to stop. She would get up and walk them there personally if she had to—and summer school. How long had the teachers been saying that they needed summer school? And she would check homework—every night. And P.T.A. Sonya wouldn't be little forever—she'd have no more excuses for missing those meetings in the evening. Junior high; high school; college—none of them stayed little forever. And then on to good jobs in insurance companies and the post office, even doctors or lawyers. Yes, that's what would happen to her babies.

The play was approaching its last act, and all the people seemed to have thought they were sleeping. *I have had a most rare vision. I have had a dream, past the wit of man to say what dream it was . . .* In the last scene the cast invited the audience to come up on stage and join them in the wedding dance that was played to rock music. The children wanted to jump up and join them, but Cora held them back. "No, no, next time!" she said, not wanting their clothes to be seen under the bright lights. The participants from the audience sat down crosslegged on the stage and the little fairy man pranced between them:

> If we shadows have offended,
> Think but this, and all is mended:
> That you have but slumber'd here,
> While these visions did appear.
> And this weak and idle theme,
> No more yielding but a dream . . .

Cora applauded until her hands tingled, and felt a strange sense of emptiness now that it was over. Oh, if they would only do it again. She let the children jump around their seats and dance to the music that continued after the play was over. Cora went down the row to Kiswana and grabbed her hand.

"Thanks so much—it was wonderful."

CORA LEE

Kiswana was slightly taken aback by this burst of emotion from the woman. "I knew you'd like it, and see how good the kids were."

"Oh, yes, it was great. I'm gonna bring them back again."

"Well, if things work out, he's planning to produce another one next year."

"We'll be here," Cora said emphatically, taking the baby from Kiswana. "Was she too much?"

"No, she's precious. Look, I'm not going back right now. I want to run and congratulate Abshu. You'll be okay?"

"Sure, and please tell him I thought it was wonderful."

"I will. See you later."

Cora and her family moved home through the moist summer night, and she smiled as the children chattered and tried to imitate some of the antics they had seen.

"Mama," Sammy pulled on her arm, "Shakespeare's black?"

"Not yet," she said softly, remembering she had beaten him for writing the rhymes on her bathroom walls.

The long walk had tired them so there were few protests about going to bed. No one questioned it when she sponged them down and put them each into bed with a kiss—this had been a night of wonders. Cora Lee took their clothes, folded them, and put them away.

She then went through her apartment, turning off the lights and breathing in hopeful echoes of order and peace that lay in the clean house. She entered her bedroom in the dark and the shadow, who had let himself in with his key, moved in the bed. He didn't ask where they had been and she didn't care to tell him. She went over and silently peeked in the crib at her sleeping daughter and let out a long sigh. Then she turned and firmly folded her evening like gold and lavender gauze deep within the creases of her dreams, and let her clothes drop to the floor.

THE TWO

At first they seemed like such nice girls. No one could remember exactly when they had moved into Brewster. It was earlier in the year before Ben was killed—of course, it had to be before Ben's death. But no one remembered if it was in the winter or spring of that year that the two had come. People often came and went on Brewster Place like a restless night's dream, moving in and out in the dark to avoid eviction notices or neighborhood bulletins about the dilapidated condition of their furnishings. So it wasn't until the two were clocked leaving in the mornings and returning in the evenings at regular intervals that it was quietly absorbed that they now claimed Brewster as home. And Brewster waited, cautiously prepared to claim them, because you never knew about young women, and obviously single at that. But when no wild music or drunken friends careened out of the corner building on weekends, and especially, when no slightly eager husbands were encouraged to linger around that first-floor apartment and run errands for them, a suspended sigh of relief floated around the two when they dumped their garbage, did their shopping, and headed for the morning bus.

The women of Brewster had readily accepted the lighter, skinny one. There wasn't much threat in her timid mincing walk and the slightly protruding teeth she seemed so eager to show everyone in her bell-like good mornings and evenings. Breaths were held a little longer in the direction of the short dark one—too pretty, and too much behind. And she insisted on wearing those thin Qiana dresses that the summer breeze molded against the maddening rhythm of the twenty pounds of rounded flesh that she swung steadily down the street. Through slitted eyes, the women watched their men watching her pass, knowing the bastards were praying for a wind. But since she seemed oblivious to whether these supplications went answered, their sighs settled around her shoulders too. Nice girls.

And so no one even cared to remember exactly when they had moved into Brewster Place, until the rumor started. It had first spread through the block like a sour odor that's only faintly perceptible and easily ignored until it starts growing in strength from the dozen mouths it had been lying in, among clammy gums and scum-coated teeth. And then it was everywhere—lining the mouths and whitening the lips of everyone as they wrinkled up their noses at its pervading smell, unable to pinpoint the source or time of its initial arrival. Sophie could—she had been there.

It wasn't that the rumor had actually begun with Sophie. A rumor needs no true parent. It only needs a willing carrier, and it found one in Sophie. She had been there—on one of those August evenings when the sun's absence is a mockery because the heat leaves the air so heavy it presses the naked skin down on your body, to the point that a sheet becomes unbearable and sleep impossible. So most of Brewster was outside that night when the two had come in together, probably from one of those air-conditioned movies downtown, and had greeted the ones who were loitering around their building. And they had started up the steps when the skinny one tripped over a child's ball and the darker one had grabbed her by the arm and around the waist to break her fall. "Careful, don't wanna lose you now." And the two of them had laughed into each other's eyes and went into the building.

The smell had begun there. It outlined the image of the stumbling woman and the one who had broken her fall. Sophie and a few other women sniffed at the spot and then, perplexed, silently looked at each other. Where had they seen that before? They had often laughed and touched each other—held each other in joy or its dark twin—but where had they seen *that* before? It came to them as the scent drifted down the steps and entered their nostrils on the way to their inner mouths. They had seen that—done that—with their men. That shared moment of invisible communion reserved for two and hidden from the rest of the world behind laughter or tears or a touch. In the days before babies, miscarriages, and other broken dreams, after stolen caresses in barn stalls and cotton houses, after intimate walks from church and secret kisses with boys who were now long forgotten or permanently fixed in their lives—that was where. They could almost feel the odor moving about in their mouths, and they slowly knitted themselves together and let it out into the air like a yellow mist that began to cling to the bricks on Brewster.

So it got around that the two in 312 were *that* way. And they had seemed like such nice girls. Their regular exits and entrances to the block were viewed with a jaundiced eye. The quiet that rested around their door on the weekends hinted of all sorts of secret rituals, and their friendly indifference to the men on the street was an insult to the women as a brazen flaunting of unnatural ways.

Since Sophie's apartment windows faced theirs from across the air shaft, she became the official watchman for the block, and her opinions were deferred to whenever the two came up in conversation. Sophie took her position seriously and was constantly alert for any telltale signs that might creep out around their drawn shades, across from which she kept a religious vigil. An entire week of drawn shades was evidence enough to send her flying around with reports that as soon as it got dark they pulled their shades down and put on the lights. Heads nodded in knowing unison—a definite sign. If doubt was voiced with a "But I pull my shades down at night too," a whispered "Yeah, but you're not *that* way" was argument enough to win them over.

Sophie watched the lighter one dumping their garbage,

and she went outside and opened the lid. Her eyes darted over the crushed tin cans, vegetable peelings, and empty chocolate chip cookie boxes. What do they do with all them chocolate chip cookies? It was surely a sign, but it would take some time to figure that one out. She saw Ben go into their apartment, and she waited and blocked his path as he came out, carrying his toolbox.

"What ya see?" She grabbed his arm and whispered wetly in his face.

Ben stared at her squinted eyes and drooping lips and shook his head slowly. "Uh, uh, uh, it was terrible."

"Yeah?" She moved in a little closer.

"Worst busted faucet I seen in my whole life." He shook her hand off his arm and left her standing in the middle of the block.

"You old sop bucket," she muttered, as she went back up on her stoop. A broken faucet, huh? Why did they need to use so much water?

Sophie had plenty to report that day. Ben had said it was terrible in there. No, she didn't know exactly what he had seen, but you can imagine—and they did. Confronted with the difference that had been thrust into their predictable world, they reached into their imaginations and, using an ancient pattern, weaved themselves a reason for its existence. Out of necessity they stitched all of their secret fears and lingering childhood nightmares into this existence, because even though it was deceptive enough to try and look as they looked, talk as they talked, and do as they did, it had to have some hidden stain to invalidate it—it was impossible for them both to be right. So they leaned back, supported by the sheer weight of their numbers and comforted by the woven barrier that kept them protected from the yellow mist that enshrouded the two as they came and went on Brester Place.

Lorraine was the first to notice the change in the people on Brewster Place. She was a shy but naturally friendly woman who got up early, and had read the morning paper and done fifty sit-ups before it was time to leave for work. She came out of her apartment eager to start her day by greeting any of her neighbors who were outside. But she noticed that some of the people who had spoken to her before made a point of having something else to do with their eyes when she passed, although she could almost feel them staring at her back as she moved on. The ones who still spoke only did so after an uncomfortable pause, in which they seemed to be peering through her before they begrudged her a good morning or evening. She wondered if it was all in her mind and she thought about mentioning it to Theresa, but she didn't want to be accused of being too sensitive again. And how would Tee even notice anything like that anyway? She had a lousy attitude and hardly ever spoke to people. She stayed in that bed until the last moment and rushed out of the house fogged-up and grumpy, and she was used to being stared at—by men at least—because of her body.

Lorraine thought about these things as she came up the block from work, carrying a large paper bag. The group of women on her stoop parted silently and let her pass.

"Good evening," she said, as she climbed the steps.

Sophie was standing on the top step and tried to peek into the bag. "You been shopping, huh? What ya buy?" It was almost an accusation.

"Groceries." Lorraine shielded the top of the bag from view and squeezed past her with a confused frown. She saw Sophie throw a knowing glance to the others at the bottom of the stoop. What was wrong with this old woman? Was she crazy or something?

Lorraine went into her apartment. Theresa was sitting by the window, reading a copy of *Mademoiselle*. She glanced up from her magazine. "Did you get my chocolate chip cookies?"

"Why good evening to you, too, Tee. And how was my day? Just wonderful." She sat the bag down on the couch. "The little Baxter boy brought in a puppy for show-and-tell, and the damn thing pissed all over the floor and then proceeded to chew the heel off my shoe, but, yes, I managed to hobble to the store and bring you your chocolate chip cookies."

Oh, Jesus, Theresa thought, she's got a bug up her ass tonight.

"Well, you should speak to Mrs. Baxter. She ought to train her kid better than that." She didn't wait for Lorraine to stop laughing before she tried to stretch her good mood. "Here, I'll put those things away. Want me to make dinner so you can rest? I only worked half a day, and the most tragic thing that went down was a broken fingernail and that got caught in my typewriter."

Lorraine followed Theresa into the kitchen. "No, I'm not really tired, and fair's fair, you cooked last night. I didn't mean to tick off like that; it's just that . . . well, Tee, have you noticed that people aren't as nice as they used to be?"

Theresa stiffened. Oh, God, here she goes again. "What people, Lorraine? Nice in what way?"

"Well, the people in this building and on the street. No one hardly speaks anymore. I mean, I'll come in and say good evening—and just silence. It wasn't like that when we first moved in. I don't know, it just makes you wonder; that's all. What are they thinking?"

"I personally don't give a shit what they're thinking. And their good evenings don't put any bread on my table."

"Yeah, but you didn't see the way that woman looked at me out there. They must feel something or know something. They probably—"

"They, they, they!" Theresa exploded. "You know, I'm not starting up with this again, Lorraine. Who in the hell are they? And where in the hell are we? Living in some dump of a building in this God-forsaken part of town around a bunch of ignorant niggers with the cotton still under their fingernails because of you and your theys. They knew something in Linden Hills, so I gave up an apartment for you that I'd been in for the last four years. And then they knew in Park

Heights, and you made me so miserable there we had to leave. Now these mysterious theys are on Brewster Place. Well, look out that window, kid. There's a big wall down that block, and this is the end of the line for me. I'm not moving anymore, so if that's what you're working yourself up to—save it!"

When Theresa became angry she was like a lump of smoldering coal, and her fierce bursts of temper always unsettled Lorraine.

"You see, that's why I didn't want to mention it." Lorraine began to pull at her fingers nervously. "You're always flying up and jumping to conclusions—no one said anything about moving. And I didn't know your life has been so miserable since you met me. I'm sorry about that," she finished tearfully.

Theresa looked at Lorraine, standing in the kitchen door like a wilted leaf, and she wanted to throw something at her. Why didn't she ever fight back? The very softness that had first attracted her to Lorraine was now a frequent cause for irritation. Smoked honey. That's what Lorraine had reminded her of, sitting in her office clutching that application. Dry autumn days in Georgia woods, thick bloated smoke under a beehive, and the first glimpse of amber honey just faintly darkened about the edges by the burning twigs. She had flowed just that heavily into Theresa's mind and had stuck there with a persistent sweetness.

But Theresa hadn't known then that this softness filled Lorraine up to the very middle and that she would bend at the slightest pressure, would be constantly seeking to surround herself with the comfort of everyone's goodwill, and would shrivel up at the least touch of disapproval. It was becoming a drain to be continually called upon for this nurturing and support that she just didn't understand. She had supplied it at first out of love for Lorraine, hoping that she would harden eventually, even as honey does when exposed to the cold. Theresa was growing tired of being clung to—of being the one who was leaned on. She didn't want a child—

she wanted someone who could stand toe to toe with her and be willing to slug it out at times. If they practiced that way with each other, then they could turn back to back and beat the hell out of the world for trying to invade their territory. But she had found no such sparring partner in Lorraine, and the strain of fighting alone was beginning to show on her.

"Well, if it was that miserable, I would have been gone a long time ago," she said, watching her words refresh Lorraine like a gentle shower.

"I guess you think I'm some sort of a sick paranoid, but I can't afford to have people calling my job or writing letters to my principal. You know I've already lost a position like that in Detroit. And teaching is my whole life, Tee."

"I know," she sighed, not really knowing at all. There was no danger of that ever happening on Brewster Place. Lorraine taught too far from this neighborhood for anyone here to recognize her in that school. No, it wasn't her job she feared losing this time, but their approval. She wanted to stand out there and chat and trade makeup secrets and cake recipes. She wanted to be secretary of their block association and be asked to mind their kids while they ran to the store. And none of that was going to happen if they couldn't even bring themselves to accept her good evenings.

Theresa silently finished unpacking the groceries. "Why did you buy cottage cheese? Who eats that stuff?"

"Well, I thought we should go on a diet."

"If *we* go on a diet, then you'll disappear. You've got nothing to lose but your hair."

"Oh, I don't know. I thought that we might want to try and reduce our hips or something." Lorraine shrugged playfully.

"No, thank you. We are very happy with our hips the way they are," Theresa said, as she shoved the cottage cheese to the back of the refrigerator. "And even when I lose weight, it never comes off there. My chest and arms just get smaller, and I start looking like a bottle of salad dressing."

The two women laughed, and Theresa sat down to watch Lorraine fix dinner. "You know, this behind has always been my downfall. When I was coming up in Georgia with my grandmother, the boys used to promise me penny candy if I would let them pat my behind. And I used to love those jawbreakers—you know, the kind that lasted all day and kept changing colors in your mouth. So I was glad to oblige them, because in one afternoon I could collect a whole week's worth of jawbreakers."

"Really. That's funny to you? Having some boy feeling all over you."

Theresa sucked her teeth. "We were only kids, Lorraine. You know, you remind me of my grandmother. That was one straight-laced old lady. She had a fit when my brother told her what I was doing. She called me into the smokehouse and told me in this real scary whisper that I could get pregnant from letting little boys pat my butt and that I'd end up like my cousin Willa. But Willa and I had been thick as fleas, and she had already given me a step-by-step summary of how she'd gotten into her predicament. But I sneaked around to her house that night just to double-check her story, since that old lady had seemed so earnest. 'Willa, are you sure?' I whispered through her bedroom window. 'I'm tellin' ya, Tee,' she said. 'Just keep both feet on the ground and you home free.' Much later I learned that advice wasn't too biologically sound, but it worked in Georgia because those country boys didn't have much imagination."

Theresa's laughter bounced off of Lorraine's silent, rigid back and died in her throat. She angrily tore open a pack of the chocolate chip cookies. "Yeah," she said, staring at Lorraine's back and biting down hard into the cookie, "it wasn't until I came up north to college that I found out there's a whole lot of things that a dude with a little imagination can do to you even with both feet on the ground. You see, Willa forgot to tell me not to bend over or squat or—"

"Must you!" Lorraine turned around from the stove with her teeth clenched tightly together.

"Must I what, Lorraine? Must I talk about things that are as much a part of life as eating or breathing or growing old? Why are you always so uptight about sex or men?"

"I'm not uptight about anything. I just think it's disgusting when you go on and on about—"

"There's nothing disgusting about it, Lorraine. You've never been with a man, but I've been with quite a few—some better than others. There were a couple who I still hope to this day will die a slow, painful death, but then there were some who were good to me—in and out of bed."

"If they were so great, then why are you with me?" Lorraine's lips were trembling.

"Because—" Theresa looked steadily into her eyes and then down at the cookie she was twirling on the table. "Because," she continued slowly, "you can take a chocolate chip cookie and put holes in it and attach it to your ears and call it an earring, or hang it around your neck on a silver chain and pretend it's a necklace—but it's still a cookie. See—you can toss it in the air and call it a Frisbee or even a flying saucer, if the mood hits you, and it's still just a cookie. Send it spinning on a table—like this—until it's a wonderful blur of amber and brown light that you can imagine to be a topaz or rusted gold or old crystal, but the law of gravity has got to come into play, sometime, and it's got to come to rest—sometime. Then all the spinning and pretending and hoopla is over with. And you know what you got?"

"A chocolate chip cookie," Lorraine said.

"Uh-uh." Theresa put the cookie in her mouth and winked. "A lesbian." She got up from the table. "Call me when dinner's ready, I'm going back to read." She stopped at the kitchen door. "Now, why are you putting gravy on that chicken, Lorraine? You know it's fattening."

The Brewster Place Block Association was meeting in Kiswana's apartment. People were squeezed on the sofa and coffee table and sitting on the floor. Kiswana had hung a red banner across the wall, "Today Brewster—Tomorrow America!" but few understood what that meant and even fewer cared. They were there because this girl had said that something could be done about the holes in their walls and the lack of heat that kept their children with congested lungs in the winter. Kiswana had given up trying to be heard above the voices that were competing with each other in volume and length of complaints against the landlord. This was the first time in their lives that they felt someone was taking them seriously, so all of the would-be-if-they-could-be lawyers, politicans, and Broadway actors were taking advantage of this rare opportunity to display their talents. It didn't matter if they often repeated what had been said or if their monologues held no relevance to the issues; each one fought for the space to outshine the other.

"Ben ain't got no reason to be here. He works for the landlord."

A few scattered yeahs came from around the room.

"I lives in this here block just like y'all," Ben said slowly, "And when you ain't got no heat, I ain't either. It's not my fault 'cause the man won't deliver no oil."

"But you stay so zooted all the time, you never cold no way."

"Ya know, a lot of things ain't the landlord's fault. The landlord don't throw garbage in the air shaft or break the glass in them doors."

"Yeah, and what about all them kids that be runnin' up and down the halls."

"Don't be talking 'bout my kids!" Cora Lee jumped up. "Lot of y'all got kids, too, and they no saints."

"Why you so touchy—who mentioned you?"

"But if the shoe fits, steal it from Thom McAn's."

"Wait, please." Kiswana held up her hands. "This is getting us nowhere. What we should be discussing today is staging a rent strike and taking the landlord to court."

"What we should be discussin'," Sophie leaned over and said to Mattie and Etta, "is that bad element that done moved in this block amongst decent people."

"Well, I done called the police at least a dozen times about C. C. Baker and them boys hanging in that alley, smoking them reefers, and robbing folks," Mattie said.

"I ain't talkin' 'bout them kids—I'm talkin' 'bout those two livin' 'cross from me in 312."

"What about 'em?"

"Oh, you know, Mattie," Etta said, staring straight at Sophie. "Those two girls who mind their business and never have a harsh word to say 'bout nobody—them the two you mean, right, Sophie?"

"What they doin'—livin' there like that—is wrong, and you know it." She turned to appeal to Mattie. "Now, you a Christian woman. The Good Book say that them things is an abomination against the Lord. We shouldn't be havin' that here on Brewster and the association should do something about it."

"My Bible also says in First Peter not to be a busybody in other people's matters, Sophie. And the way I see it, if they ain't botherin' with what goes on in my place, why should I bother 'bout what goes on in theirs?"

"They sinning against the Lord!" Sophie's eyes were bright and wet.

"Then let the Lord take care of it," Etta snapped. "Who appointed you?"

"That don't surprise me comin' from *you*. No, not one bit!" Sophie glared at Etta and got up to move around the room to more receptive ears.

Etta started to go after her, but Mattie held her arm. "Let that woman be. We're not here to cause no row over some of her stupidness."

"The old prune pit," Etta spit out. "She oughta be glad them two girls are that way. That's one less bed she gotta worry 'bout pullin' Jess out of this year. I didn't see her thumpin' no Bible when she beat up that woman from Mobile she caught him with last spring."

"Etta, I'd never mention it in front of Sophie 'cause I hate the way she loves to drag other people's business in the street, but I can't help feelin' that what they're doing ain't quite right. How do you get that way? Is it from birth?"

"I couldn't tell you, Mattie. But I seen a lot of it in my time and the places I've been. They say they just love each other—who knows?"

Mattie was thinking deeply. "Well, I've loved women, too. There was Miss Eva and Ciel, and even as ornery as you can get, I've loved you practically all my life."

"Yeah, but it's different with them."

"Different how?"

"Well . . ." Etta was beginning to feel uncomfortable. "They love each other like you'd love a man or a man would love you—I guess."

"But I've loved some women deeper than I ever loved any man," Mattie was pondering. "And there been some women who loved me more and did more for me than any man ever did."

"Yeah." Etta thought for a moment. "I can second that, but it's still different, Mattie. I can't exactly put my finger on it, but . . ."

"Maybe it's not so different," Mattie said, almost to herself. "Maybe that's why some women get so riled up about it, 'cause they know deep down it's not so different after all." She looked at Etta. "It kinda gives you a funny feeling when you think about it that way, though."

"Yeah, it does," Etta said, unable to meet Mattie's eyes.

Lorraine was climbing the dark narrow stairway up to Kiswana's apartment. She had tried to get Theresa to come, but she had wanted no part of it. "A tenants' meeting for what? The damn street needs to be condemned." She knew Tee blamed her for having to live in a place like Brewster, but she could at least try to make the best of things and get involved with the community. That was the problem with so many black people—they just sat back and complained while the whole world tumbled down around their heads. And grabbing an attitude and thinking you were better than these people just because a lot of them were poor and uneducated wouldn't help, either. It just made you seem standoffish, and Lorraine wanted to be liked by the people around her. She couldn't live the way Tee did, with her head stuck in a book all the time. Tee didn't seem to need anyone. Lorraine often wondered if she even needed her.

But if you kept to yourself all the time, people started to wonder, and then they talked. She couldn't afford to have people talking about her, Tee should understand that—she knew from the way they had met. Understand. It was funny because that was the first thing she had felt about her when she handed Tee her application. She had said to herself, I feel that I can talk to this woman, I can tell her why I lost my job in Detroit, and she will understand. And she had understood, but then slowly all that had stopped. Now Lorraine was made to feel awkward and stupid about her fears and thoughts. Maybe Tee was right and she was too sensitive, but there was a big difference between being personnel director for the Board of Education and a first-grade teacher. Tee didn't threaten their files and payroll accounts but, somehow, she, Lorraine, threatened their children. Her heart tightened when she thought about that. The worst thing she had ever wanted to do to a child was to slap the spit out of the little Baxter boy for pouring glue in her hair, and even that had only been for a fleeting moment. Didn't Tee understand that if she lost this job, she wouldn't be so lucky the next time? No, she didn't understand that or anything else about her. She never wanted to bother with anyone except those weirdos at that club she went to, and Lorraine hated them. They were coarse and bitter, and made fun of people who weren't like them. Well, she wasn't like them either. Why should she feel different from the people she lived around? Black people were all in the same boat—she'd come to realize this even more since they had moved to Brewster—and if they didn't row together, they would sink together.

Lorraine finally reached the top floor; the door to Kiswana's apartment was open but she knocked before she went in. Kiswana was trying to break up an argument between a short light-skinned man and some woman who had picked up a potted plant and was threatening to hit him in the mouth. Most of the other tenants were so busy rooting for one or the other that hardly anyone noticed Lorraine when she entered. She went over and stood by Ben.

"I see there's been a slight difference of opinion here," she smiled.

"Just nigger mess, miss. Roscoe there claim that Betina ain't got no right being secretary 'cause she owe three months' rent, and she say he owe more than that and it's none of his never mind. Don't know how we got into all this. Ain't what we was talkin' 'bout, no way. Was talkin' 'bout havin' a block party to raise money for a housing lawyer."

Kiswana had rescued her Boston Fern from the woman and the two people were being pulled to opposite sides of the room. Betina pushed her way out of the door, leaving behind very loud advice about where they could put their secretary's job along with the block association, if they could find the space in that small an opening in their bodies.

Kiswana sat back down, flushed and out of breath. "Now we need someone else to take the minutes."

"Do they come with the rest of the watch?" Laughter and another series of monologues about Betina's bad-natured exit followed for the next five minutes.

Lorraine saw that Kiswana looked as if she wanted to cry. The one-step-forward–two-steps-backwards progression of the meeting was beginning to show on her face. Lorraine swallowed her shyness and raised her hand. "I'll take the minutes for you."

"Oh, thank you." Kiswana hurriedly gathered the scattered and crumpled papers and handed them to her. "Now we can get back down to business."

The room was now aware of Lorraine's presence, and there were soft murmurs from the corners, accompanied by furtive glances while a few like Sophie stared at her openly. She attempted to smile into the eyes of the people watching her, but they would look away the moment she glanced in their direction. After a couple of vain attempts her smile died, and she buried it uneasily in the papers in her hand. Lorraine tried to cover her trembling fingers by pretending to decipher Betina's smudged and misspelled notes.

"All right," Kiswana said, "now who had promised to get a stereo hooked up for the party?"

"Ain't we supposed to vote on who we wants for secretary?" Sophie's voice rose heavily in the room, and its weight smothered the other noise. All of the faces turned silently toward hers with either mild surprise or coveted satisfaction over what they knew was coming. "I mean, can anybody just waltz in here and get shoved down our throats and we don't have a say about it?"

"Look, I can just go," Lorraine said. "I just wanted to help, I—"

"No, wait." Kiswana was confused. "What vote? Nobody else wanted to do it. Did you want to take the notes?"

"She can't do it," Etta cut in, "unless we was sitting here reciting the ABC's, and we better not do that too fast. So let's just get on with the meeting."

Scattered approval came from sections of the room.

"Listen here!" Sophie jumped up to regain lost ground. "Why should a decent woman get insulted and y'll take sides with the likes of them?" Her finger shot out like a pistol, which she swung between Etta and Lorraine.

Etta rose from her seat. "Who do you think you're talkin' to, you old hen's ass? I'm as decent as you are, and I'll come over there and lam you in the mouth to prove it!"

Etta tried to step across the coffee table, but Mattie caught her by the back of the dress; Etta turned, tried to shake her off, and tripped over the people in front of her. Sophie picked up a statue and backed up into the wall with it slung over her shoulder like a baseball bat. Kiswana put her head in her hands and groaned. Etta had taken off her high-heeled shoe and was waving the spiked end at Sophie over the shoulders of the people who were holding her back.

"That's right! That's right!" Sophie screamed. "Pick on me! Sure, I'm the one who goes around doin' them filthy, unnatural things right under your noses. Every one of you knows it; everybody done talked about it, not just me!" Her head moved around the room like a trapped animal's. "And any woman—any woman who defends that kind of thing just better be watched. That's all I gotta say—where there's smoke, there's fire, Etta Johnson!"

Etta stopped struggling against the arms that were holding her, and her chest was heaving in rapid spasms as she threw Sophie a look of wilting hate, but she remained silent. And no other woman in the room dared to speak as they moved an extra breath away from each other. Sophie turned toward Lorraine, who had twisted the meeting's notes into a mass of shredded paper. Lorraine kept her back straight, but her hands and mouth were moving with a will of their own. She stood like a fading spirit before the ebony statue that Sophie pointed at her like a crucifix.

"Movin' into our block causin' a disturbance with your nasty ways. You ain't wanted here!"

"What have any of you ever seen me do except leave my house and go to work like the rest of you? Is it disgusting for me to speak to each one of you that I meet in the street, even when you don't answer me back? Is that my crime?" Lorraine's voice sank like a silver dagger into their consciences, and there was an uneasy stirring in the room.

"Don't stand there like you a Miss Innocent," Sophie whispered hoarsely. "I'll tell ya what I seen!"

Her eyes leered around the room as they waited with a courtroom hush for her next words.

"I wasn't gonna mention something so filthy, but you forcin' me." She ran her tongue over her parched lips and narrowed her eyes at Lorraine. "You forgot to close your shades last night, and I saw the two of you!"

The silence in the room tightened into a half-gasp.

"There you was, standin' in the bathroom door, drippin'

wet and as naked and shameless as you please . . ."

It had become so quiet it was now painful.

"Calling to the other one to put down her book and get you a clean towel. Standin' in that bathroom door with your naked behind. I saw it—I did!"

Their chests were beginning to burn from a lack of air as they waited for Lorraine's answer, but before the girl could open her mouth, Ben's voice snaked from behind her like a lazy breeze.

"Guess *you* get out the tub with your clothes on, Sophie. Must make it mighty easy on Jess's eyes."

The laughter that burst out of their lungs was such a relief that eyes were watery. The room laid its head back and howled in gratitude to Ben for allowing it to breathe again. Sophie's rantings could not be heard above the wheezing, coughing, and backslapping that now went on.

Lorraine left the apartment and grasped the stairway railing, trying to keep the bile from rising into her throat. Ben followed her outside and gently touched her shoulder.

"Miss, you all right?"

She pressed her lips tightly together and nodded her head. The lightness of his touch brought tears to her eyes, and she squeezed them shut.

"You sure? You look 'bout ready to keel over."

Lorraine shook her head jerkily and sank her nails deeply into her palm as she brought her hand to her mouth. I mustn't speak, she thought. If I open my mouth, I'll scream. Oh, God, I'll scream or I'll throw up, right here, in front of this nice old man. The thought of the churned up bits of her breakfast and lunch pouring out of her mouth and splattering on Ben's trouser legs suddenly struck her as funny, and she fought an overwhelming desire to laugh. She trembled violently as the creeping laughter tried to deceive her into parting her lips.

Ben's face clouded over as he watched the frail body that was so bravely struggling for control. "Come on now, I'll take you home." And he tried to lead her down the steps.

She shook her head in a panic. She couldn't let Tee see her like this. If she says anything smart to me now, I'll kill her, Lorraine thought. I'll pick up a butcher knife and plunge it into her face, and then I'll kill myself and let them find us there. The thought of all those people in Kiswana's apartment standing over their bleeding bodies was strangely comforting, and she began to breathe more easily.

"Come on now," Ben urged quietly, and edged her toward the steps.

"I can't go home." She barely whispered.

"It's all right, you ain't gotta—come on."

And she let him guide her down the stairs and out into the late September evening. He took her to the building that was nearest to the wall on Brewster Place and then down the outside steps to a door with a broken dirty screen. Ben unlocked the door and led her into his damp underground rooms.

He turned on the single light bulb that was hanging from the ceiling by a thick black cord and pulled out a chair for her at the kitchen table, which was propped up against the wall. Lorraine sat down, grateful to be able to take the weight off of her shaky knees. She didn't acknowledge his apologies as he took the half-empty wine bottle and cracked cup from the table. He brushed off the crumbs while two fat brown roaches raced away from the wet cloth.

"I'm makin' tea," he said, without asking her if she wanted any. He placed a blackened pot of water on the hot plate at the edge of the counter, then found two cups in the cabinet that still had their handles intact. Ben put the strong black tea he had brewed in front of her and brought her a spoon and a crumpled pound bag of sugar. Lorraine took three heaping teaspoons of sugar and stirred the tea, holding her face over the steam. Ben waited for her face to register the effects of the hot sweet liquid.

"I liked you from first off," he said shyly, and seeing her smile, he continued. "You remind me lots of my little girl." Ben reached into his hip pocket and took out a frayed billfold and handed her a tiny snapshot.

Lorraine tilted the picture toward the light. The face stamped on the celluloid paper bore absolutely no resemblance to her at all. His daughter's face was oval and dark, and she had a large flat nose and a tiny rounded mouth. She handed the picture back to Ben and tried to cover her confusion.

"I know what you thinkin'," Ben said, looking at the face in his hands. "But she had a limp—my little girl. Was a breech baby, and the midwife broke her foot when she was birthed and it never came back right. Always kinda cripped along—but a sweet child." He frowned deeply into the picture and paused, then looked up at Lorraine. "When I seen you—the way you'd walk up the street all timid-like and tryin' to be nice to these-here folks and the look on your face when some of 'em was just downright rude—you kinda broke up in here." He motioned toward his chest. "And you just sorta limped along inside. That's when I thought of my baby."

Lorraine gripped the teacup with both hands, but the tears still squeezed through the compressed muscles in her eyes. They slowly rolled down her face but she wouldn't release the cup to wipe them away.

"My father," she said, staring into the brown liquid, "kicked me out of the house when I was seventeen years old. He found a letter one of my girlfriends had written me, and when I wouldn't lie about what it meant, he told me to get out and leave behind everything that he had ever bought me. He said he wanted to burn them." She looked up to see the expression on Ben's face, but it kept swimming under the tears in her eyes. "So I walked out of his home with only the clothes on my back. I moved in with one of my cousins, and I worked at night in a bakery to put myself through college. I would send him a birthday card each year, and he always returned them unopened. After a while I stopped putting my return address on the envelopes so he couldn't send them back. I guess he burned those too." She sniffed the mucus up into her nose. "I still send those cards like that—without a return address. That way I can believe that, maybe, one year before he dies, he'll open them."

Ben got up and gave her a piece of toilet paper to blow her nose in.

"Where's your daughter now, Mr. Ben?"

"For me?" Ben sighed deeply. "Just like you—livin' in a world with no address."

They finished their tea in silence and Lorraine got up to go.

"There's no way to thank you, so I won't try."

"I'd be right hurt if you did." Ben patted her arm. "Now come back anytime you got a mind to. I got nothing, but you welcome to all of that. Now how many folks is that generous?"

Lorraine smiled, leaned over, and kissed him on the cheek. Ben's face lit up the walls of the dingy basement. He closed the door behind her, and at first her "Good night, Mr. Ben" tinkled like crystal bells in his mind. Crystal bells that grew larger and louder, until their sound was distorted in his ears and he almost believed that she had said "Good night, Daddy Ben"—no—"Mornin' Daddy Ben, mornin' Daddy Ben, mornin' . . .' Ben's saliva began to taste like sweating tin, and he ran a trembling hand over his stubbled face and rushed to the corner where he had shoved the wine bottle. The bells had begun almost to deafen him and he shook his head to relieve the drumming pain inside of his ears. He knew what was coming next, and he didn't dare waste time by pouring the wine into a cup. He lifted the bottle up to his mouth and sucked at it greedily, but it was too late. *Swing low, sweet chariot.* The song had started—the whistling had begun.

It started low, from the end of his gut, and shrilled its way up into his ears and shattered the bells, sending glass shards flying into a heart that should have been so scarred from old piercings that there was no flesh left to bleed. But the glass splinters found some minute, untouched place—as they always did—and tore the heart and let the whistling in. And now Ben would have to drink faster and longer, because the melody would now ride on his body's blood like a cancer and poison everywhere it touched. *Swing low, sweet chariot.* It mustn't get to his brain. He had a few more seconds before it got to his brain and killed him. He had to be drunk before the poison crept up his neck muscles, past his mouth, on the way to his brain. If he was drunk, then he could let it out—sing it out into the air before it touched his brain, caused him to remember. *Swing low, sweet chariot.* He couldn't die there under the ground like some animal. Oh, God, please make him drunk. And he promised—he'd never go that long without a drink again. It was just the meeting and then that girl that had kept him from it this long, but he swore it would never happen again—just please, God, make him drunk.

The alcohol began to warm Ben's body, and he felt his head begin to get numb and heavy. He almost sobbed out his thanks for this redeeming answer to his prayers, because the whistling had just reached his throat and he was able to open his mouth and slobber the words out into the room. The saliva was dripping from the corners of his mouth because he had to take huge gulps of wine between breaths, but he sang on—drooling and humming—because to sing was salvation, to sing was to empty the tune from his blood, to sing was to unremember Elvira, and his daughter's "Mornin', Daddy Ben" as she dragged her twisted foot up his front porch with that song hitting her in the back.
Swing low
   "Mornin', Ben. Mornin', Elvira."
Sweet chariot
   The red pick-up truck stopped in front of Ben's yard.
Comin' for to carry me home
   His daughter got out of the passenger side and began to limp toward the house.
Swing low
   Elvira grinned into the creviced face of the white man sitting in the truck with tobacco stains in the corner of his

mouth. "Mornin', Mr. Clyde. Right nice day, ain't it, sir?"
Sweet chariot

Ben watched his daughter come through the gate with her eyes on the ground, and she slowly climbed up on the porch. She took each step at a time, and her shoes grated against the rough boards. She finally turned her beaten eyes into his face, and what was left of his soul to crush was taken care of by the bell-like voice that greeted them. "Mornin', Daddy Ben. Mornin', Mama."

"Mornin', baby," Ben mumbled with his jaws tight.
Swing low

"How's things up at the house?" Elvira asked. "My little girl do a good job for you yesterday?"
Sweet chariot

"Right fine, Elvira. Got that place clean as a skinned rat. How's y'all's crops comin'?"

"Just fine, Mr. Clyde, sir. Just fine. We sure appreciate that extra land you done rented us. We bringin' in more than enough to break even. Yes, sir, just fine."

The man laughed, showing the huge gaps between his to-bacco-rotted teeth. "Glad to do it. Y'all some of my best tenants. I likes keepin' my people happy. If you needs somethin', let me know."

"Sure will, Mr. Clyde, sir."

"Aw right, see y'all next week. Be by the regular time to pick up the gal."

"She be ready, sir."

The man started up the motor on the truck, and the tune that he whistled as he drove off remained in the air long after the dust had returned to the ground. Elvira grinned and waved until the red of the truck had disappeared over the horizon. Then she simultaneously dropped her arm and smile and turned toward her daughter. "Don't just stand there gawkin'. Get in the house—your breakfast been ready."

"Yes, Mama."

When the screen door had slammed shut, Elvira snapped

her head around to Ben. "Nigger, what is wrong with you? Ain't you heared Mr. Clyde talkin' to you, and you standin' there like a hunk of stone. You better get some sense in you head 'fore I knock some in you!"

Ben stood with his hands in his pockets, staring at the tracks in the dirt where the truck had been. He kept balling his fists up in his overalls until his nails dug into his palms.

"It ain't right, Elvira. It just ain't right and you know it."

"What ain't right?" The woman stuck her face into his and he backed up a few steps. "That that gal work and earn her keep like the rest of us? She can't go to the fields, but she can clean house, and she'll do it! I see it's better you keep your mouth shut 'cause when it's open, ain't nothin' but stupidness comin' out." She turned her head and brushed him off as she would a fly, then headed toward the door of the house.

"She came to us, Elvira." There was a leaden sadness in Ben's voice. "She came to us a long time ago."

The thin woman spun around with her face twisted into an airless knot. "She came to us with a bunch of lies 'bout Mr. Clyde 'cause she's too damn lazy to work. Why would a decent widow man want to mess with a little black nothin' like her? No, anything to get out of work—just like you."

"Why she gotta spend the night then?" Ben turned his head slowly toward her. "Why he always make her spend the night up there alone with him?"

"Why should he make an extra trip just to bring her tail home when he pass this way every Saturday mornin' on the way to town? If she wasn't lame, she could walk it herself after she finish work. But the man nice enough to drop her home, and you want to bad-mouth him along with that lyin' hussy."

"After she came to us, you remember I borrowed Tommy Boy's wagon and went to get her that Friday night. I told ya what Mr. Clyde told me. 'She ain't finished yet, Ben.' Just like that—'She ain't finished yet.' And then standin' there whistlin' while I went out the back gate." Ben's nails dug deeper into his palms.

"So!" Elvira's voice was shrill. "So it's a big house. It ain't like this shit you got us livin' in. It take her longer to do things than most folks. You know that, so why stand there carryin' on like it mean more than that?"

"She ain't finished yet, Ben." Ben shook his head slowly. "If I was half a man I woulda—"

Elvira came across the porch and sneered into his face. "If you was half a man, you coulda given me more babies and we woulda had some help workin' this land instead of a half-grown woman we gotta carry the load for. And if you was even quarter a man, we wouldn't be a bunch of miserable sharecroppers on someone else's land—but we is, Ben. And I'll be damned if I see the little bit we got taken away 'cause you believe that gal's lowdown lies! So when Mr. Clyde come by here, you speak—hear me? And you act as grateful as your pitiful ass should be for the favors he done us."

Ben felt a slight dampness in his hands because his fingernails had broken through the skin of his palms and the blood was seeping around his cuticles. He looked at Elvira's dark braided head and wondered why he didn't take his hands out of his pockets and stop the bleeding by pressing them around it. Just lock his elbows on her shoulders and place one hand on each side of her temples and then in toward each other until the blood stopped. His big calloused hands on the bones of her skull pressing in and in, like you would with a piece of dark cloth to cover the wounds on your body and clot the blood. Or he could simply go into the house and take his shotgun and press his palms around the trigger and handle, emptying the bullets into her sagging breasts just long enough—just pressing hard enough—to stop his palms from bleeding.

But the gram of truth in her words was heavy enough to weigh his hands down in his pockets and keep his feet nailed to the wooden planks in the porch, and the wounds healed over by themselves. Ben discovered that if he sat up drinking all night Friday, he could stand on the porch Saturday morning and smile at the man who whistled as he dropped his lame daughter home. And he could look into her beaten eyes and believe that she had lied.

The girl disappeared one day, leaving behind a note saying that she loved them very much, but she knew that she had been a burden and she understood why they had made her keep working at Mr. Clyde's house. But she felt that if she had to earn her keep that way, she might as well go to Memphis where the money was better.

Elvira ran and bragged to the neighbors that their daughter was now working in a rich house in Memphis. And she was making out awful well because she always sent plenty of money home. Ben would stare at the envelopes with no return address, and he found that if he drank enough every time a letter came, he could silence the bell-like voice that came chiming out of the open envelope—"Mornin' Daddy Ben, mornin' Daddy Ben, mornin' . . ." And then if he drank enough every day he could bear the touch of Elvira's body in the bed beside him at night and not have his sleep stolen by the image of her lying there with her head caved in or her chest ripped apart by shotgun shells.

But even after they lost the sharecropping contract and Elvira left him for a man who farmed near the levee and Ben went north and took a job on Brewster, he still drank—long after he could remember why. He just knew that whenever he saw a mailman, the crystal bells would start, and then that strange whistling that could shatter them, sending them on that deadly journey toward his heart.

He never dreamed it would happen on a Sunday. The mailman didn't run on Sundays, so he had felt safe. He hadn't counted on that girl sounding so much like the bells when she left his place tonight. But it was okay, he had gotten drunk in time, and he would never take such a big chance again. No, Lord, you pulled me through this time, and I ain't pressin' your mercy no more. Ben stumbled around his shadowy damp rooms, singing now at the top of his voice. The low, trembling melody of "Swing Low, Sweet Chariot" passed through his greasy windows and up into the late summer air.

Lorraine had walked home slowly, thinking about the old man and the daughter who limped. When she came to her stoop, she brushed past her neighbors with her head up and didn't bother to speak.

Theresa got off the uptown bus and turned the corner into Brewster Place. She was always irritable on Friday evenings because they had to do payroll inventories at the office. Her neck ached from bending over endless lists of computer printouts. What did that damn Board of Education think—someone in accounting was going to sneak one of their relatives on the payroll? The biggies had been doing that for years, but they lay awake at night, thinking of ways to keep the little guys from cashing in on it too. There was something else that had been turning uncomfortably in her mind for the last few weeks, and just today it had lain still long enough for her to pinpoint it—Lorraine was changing. It wasn't exactly anything that she had said or done, but Theresa sensed a firmness in her spirit that hadn't been there before. She was speaking up more—yes, that was it—whether the subject was the evening news or bus schedules or the proper way to hem a dress. Lorraine wasn't deferring to her anymore. And she wasn't apologizing for seeing things differently from Theresa.

Why did that bother her? Didn't she want Lorraine to start standing up for herself? To stop all that sniveling and hand-wringing every time Theresa raised her voice? Weren't things the way she had wanted them to be for the last five years? What nagged at Theresa more than the change was the fact that she was worrying about it. She had actually thought about picking a fight just to see how far she could push her— push her into what? Oh, God, I must be sick, she thought.

No, it was that old man—that's what it was. Why was Lorraine spending so much time with that drunk? They didn't have a damn thing in common. What could he be telling her, doing for her, that was causing this? She had tried—she truly had—to get Lorraine to show some backbone. And now some ignorant country winehead was doing in a few weeks what she couldn't do for the last five years.

Theresa was mulling this over when a little girl sped past her on skates, hit a crack in the sidewalk, and fell. She went to walk around the child, who looked up with tears in her eyes and stated simply, "Miss, I hurt myself." She said it with such a tone of wonder and disappointment that Theresa smiled. Kids lived in such an insulated world, where the smallest disturbance was met with cries of protest. Oh, sweetheart, she thought, just live on and you'll wish many a day that the biggest problem in your life would be a scraped knee. But she was still just a little girl, and right now she wanted an audience for her struggle with this uninvited disaster.

Theresa bent down beside her and clucked her teeth loudly. "Oh, you did? Let's see." She helped her off the ground and made an exaggerated fuss over the scraped knee.

"It's bleeding!" The child's voice rose in horror.

Theresa looked at the tiny specks of blood that were beading up on the grimy knee. "Why, it sure is." She tried to match the note of seriousness in the child's tone. "But I think we have a little time before you have to worry about a transfusion." She opened her pocketbook and took out a clean tissue. "Let's see if we can fix it up. Now, I want you to spit on this for me and I'll wipe your knee."

The girl spit on the tissue. "Is it gonna hurt?"

"No, it won't hurt. You know what my grandma used to call spit? God's iodine. Said it was the best thing for patching anything up—except maybe a broken leg."

She steadied the girl's leg and gently dabbed at the dirty knee. "See, it's all coming off. I guess you're gonna live." She smiled.

The child looked at her knee with a solemn face. "I think it needs a Band-Aid."

Theresa laughed. "Well, you're out of luck with me. But you go on home and see if your mama has one for you—if you can remember which knee it was by then."

"What are you doing to her?" The voice pierced the air between the child and Theresa. She looked up and saw a woman rushing toward them. The woman grabbed the child to her side. "What's going on here?" Her voice was just half an octave too high.

Theresa stood up and held out the dirty and bloody tissue. "She scraped her knee." The words fell like dead weights. "What in the hell did you think I was doing?" She refused to let the woman avoid her eyes, enjoying every minute of her cringing embarrassment.

"Mama, I need a Band-Aid, you got a Band-Aid?" The child tugged on her arm.

"Yes, yes, honey, right away." The woman was glad to have an excuse to look down. "Thank you very much," she said, as she hurried the child away. "She's always so clumsy. I've told her a million times to be careful on those skates, but you know . . ."

"Yeah, right," Theresa said, watching them go. "I know." She balled the tissue in her hand and quickly walked into the building. She slammed the apartment door open and heard Lorraine running water in the bathroom.

"Is that you, Tee?"

"Yeah," she called out, and then thought, No, it's not me. It's not me at all. Theresa paced between the kitchen and living room and then realized that she still had the tissue. She threw it into the kitchen garbage and turned on the faucet to its fullest pressure and started washing her hands. She kept lathering and rinsing them, but they still felt unclean. Son-of-a-bitch, she thought, son-of-a-fucking-bitch! She roughly dried her hands with some paper towels and fought the impulse to wash them again by starting dinner early. She kept her hands moving quickly, chopping more onions, celery, and green peppers than she really needed. She vigorously seasoned the ground beef, jabbing the wooden spoon repeatedly into the red meat.

When she stopped to catch her breath and glanced toward the kitchen window, a pair of squinty black eyes were peering at her from the corner of a shade across the air shaft. "What the hell . . . ?" She threw down her spoon and ran over to the window.

"You wanna see what I'm doing?" The shade was pulled up with such force it went spinning on its rollers at the top of the window. The eyes disappeared from the corner of the shade across the air shaft.

"Here!" Theresa slammed the window up into its casing. "I'll even raise this so you can hear better. I'm making meat loaf, you old bat! Meat loaf!" She stuck her head out of the window. "The same way other people make it! Here, I'll show you!"

She ran back to the table and took up a handful of chopped onions and threw them at Sophie's window. "See, that's the onions. And here, here's the chopped peppers!" The diced vegetables hit against the windowpane. "Oh, yeah, I use eggs!" Two eggs flew out of the window and splattered against Sophie's panes.

Lorraine came out of the bathroom, toweling her hair. "What's all the shouting for? Who are you talking to?" She saw Theresa running back and forth across the kitchen, throwing their dinner out of the window. "Have you lost your mind?"

Theresa picked up a jar of olives. "Now, here's something *freaky* for you—olives! I put olives in my meat loaf! So run up and down the street and tell that!" The jar of olives crashed against the opposite building, barely missing Sophie's window.

"Tee, stop it!"

Theresa put her head back out the window. "Now olives are definitely weird, but you gotta take that one up with my grandmother because it's her recipe! Wait! I forgot the meat—can't have you think I would try to make meat loaf without meat." She ran back to the table and grabbed up the bowl.

"Theresa!!" Lorraine rushed into the kitchen.

"No, can't have you thinking that!" Theresa yelled as she swung back her arm to throw the bowl through Sophie's window. "You might feel I'm a *pervert* or something—someone you can't trust your damn children around!"

Lorraine caught her arm just as she went to hurl the bowl out of the window. She grabbed the bowl and shoved Theresa against the wall.

"Look," Lorraine said, pressing against the struggling woman, "I know you're pissed off, but ground sirloin is almost three dollars a pound!"

The look of sincere horror on Lorraine's face as she cradled the bowl of meat in her arm made Theresa giggle, and then slowly she started laughing and Lorraine nodded her head and laughed with her. Theresa laid her head back against the wall, and her plump throat vibrated from the full sounds passing through it. Lorraine let her go and put the bowl on the table. Theresa's sides were starting to ache from laughing, and she sat down in one of the kitchen chairs. Lorraine pushed the bowl a little further down the table from her, and this set them off again. Theresa laughed and rocked in the chair until tears were rolling down her cheeks. Then she crossed that fine line between laughter and tears and started to sob. Lorraine went over to her, cradled her head in her chest, and stroked her shoulders. She had no idea what had brought on all of this, but it didn't matter. It felt good to be the one who could now comfort.

The shade across the air shaft moved a fraction of an inch, and Sophie pressed one eye against her smeared and dripping windowpane. She looked at the two women holding each other and shook her head. "Um, um, um."

The next day Lorraine was on her way back from the supermarket, and she ran into Kiswana, who was coming out of their building, carrying an armful of books.

"Hi," she greeted Lorraine, "you sure have a full load there."

"Well, we ran out of vegetables last night." Lorraine smiled. "So I picked up a little extra today."

"You know, we haven't seen you at the meetings lately. Things are really picking up. There's going to be a block party next weekend, and we can use all the help we can get."

Lorraine stopped smiling. "Did you really think I'd come back after what happened?"

The blood rushed to Kiswana's face and she stared uncomfortably at the top of her books. "You know, I'm really sorry about that. I should have said something—after all, it was my house—but things just sort of got out of hand so quickly, I'm sorry, I . . ."

"Hey, look, I'm not blaming you or even that woman who made such a fuss. She's just a very sick lady, that's all. Her life must be very unhappy if she has to run around and try to hurt people who haven't done anything to her. But I just didn't want any more trouble, so I felt I ought to stay away."

"But the association is for all of us," Kiswana insisted, "and everyone doesn't feel the way she did. What you do is your own business, not that you're doing anything, anyway. I mean, well, two women or two guys can't live together without people talking. She could be your cousin or sister or something."

"We're not related," Lorraine said quietly.

"Well, good friends then," Kiswana stammered. "Why can't good friends just live together and people mind their own business. And even if you're not friends, even . . . well, whatever." She went on miserably, "It was my house and I'm sorry, I . . ."

Lorraine was kind enough to change the subject for her. "I see you have an armful yourself. You're heading toward the library?"

"No." Kiswana gave her a grateful smile. "I'm taking a few

classes on the weekends. My old lady is always on my back about going back to school, so I enrolled at the community college." She was almost apologetic. "But I'm only studying black history and the science of revolution, and I let her know that. But it's enough to keep her quiet."

"I think that's great. You know, I took quite a few courses in black history when I went to school in Detroit."

"Yeah, which ones?"

While they were talking, C. C. Baker and his friends loped up the block. These young men always moved in a pack, or never without two or three. They needed the others continually near to verify their existence. When they stood with their black skin, ninth-grade diplomas, and fifty-word vocabularies in front of the mirror that the world had erected and saw nothing, those other pairs of tight jeans, suede sneakers, and tinted sunglasses imaged nearby proved that they were alive. And if there was life, there could be dreams of that miracle that would one day propel them into the heaven populated by their gods—Shaft and Superfly. While they grew old awaiting that transformation they moved through the streets, insuring that they could at least be heard, if not seen, by blasting their portable cassette players and talking loudly. They continually surnamed each other Man and clutched at their crotches, readying the equipment they deemed necessary to be summoned at any moment into Superfly heaven.

The boys recognized Kiswana because her boyfriend, Abshu, was director of the community center, and Lorraine had been pointed out to them by parents or some other adult who had helped to spread the yellow mist. They spotted the two women talking to each other, and on a cue from C. C., they all slowed as they passed the stoop. C. C. Baker was greatly disturbed by the thought of a Lorraine. He knew of only one way to deal with women other than his mother. Before he had learned exactly how women gave birth, he knew how to please or punish or extract favors from them by the execution of what lay curled behind his fly. It was his lifeline to that part of his being that sheltered his self-respect. And the thought of any woman who lay beyond the length of its power was a threat.

"Hey, Swana, better watch it talkin' to that dyke—she might try to grab a tit!" C. C. called out.

"Yeah, Butch, why don't ya join the WACS and really have a field day."

Lorraine's arms tightened around her packages, and she tried to push past Kiswana and go into the building. "I'll see you later."

"No, wait." Kiswana blocked her path. "Don't let them talk to you like that. They're nothing but a bunch of punks." She called out to the leader, "C. C., why don't you just take your little dusty behind and get out of here. No one was talking to you."

The muscular tan boy spit out his cigarette and squared his shoulders. "I ain't got to do nothin'! And I'm gonna tell Abshu you need a good spankin' for taking up with a lesbo." He looked around at his reflections and preened himself in their approval. "Why don't ya come over here and I'll show ya what a real man can do." He cupped his crotch.

Kiswana's face reddened with anger. "From what I heard about you, C. C., I wouldn't even feel it."

His friends broke up with laughter, and when he turned around to them, all he could see mirrored was respect for the girl who had beat him at the dozens. Lorraine smiled at the absolutely lost look on his face. He curled his lips back into a snarl and tried to regain lost ground by attacking what instinct told him was the weaker of the two.

"Ya laughing at me, huh, freak? I oughta come over there and stick my fist in your cunt-eatin' mouth!"

"You'll have to come through me first, so just try it." Kiswana put her books on the stoop.

"Aw, Man, come on. Don't waste your time." His friends pulled at his arm. "She ain't nothing but a woman."

"I oughta go over there and slap that bitch in her face and teach her a lesson."

"Hey, Man, lay light, lay light," one whispered in his ear. "That's Abshu's woman, and that big dude don't mind kickin' ass."

C. C. did an excellent job of allowing himself to be reluctantly pulled away from Kiswana, but she wasn't fooled and had already turned to pick up her books. He made several jerky motions with his fist and forefinger at Lorraine.

"I'm gonna remember this, Butch!"

Theresa had watched the entire scene out of the window and had been ready to run out and help Kiswana if the boy had come up on the stoop. That was just like Lorraine to stand there and let someone else take up for her. Well, maybe she'd finally learned her lesson about these ignorant nothings on Brewster Place. They weren't ever going to be accepted by these people, and there was no point in trying.

Theresa left the window and sat on the couch, pretending to be solving a crossword puzzle when Lorraine came in.

"You look a little pale. Were the prices that bad at the store today?"

"No, this heat just drains me. It's hard to believe that we're in the beginning of October." She headed straight for the kitchen.

"Yeah," Theresa said, watching her back intently. "Indian Summer and all that."

"Mmm." Lorraine dumped the bags on the table. "I'm too tired to put these away now. There's nothing perishable in there. I think I'll take some aspirin and lay down."

"Do that," Theresa said, and followed her into the bedroom. "Then you'll be rested for later. Saddle called—he and Byron are throwing a birthday party at the club, and they want us to come over."

Lorraine was looking through the top dresser drawer for her aspirin. "I'm not going over there tonight. I hate those parties."

"You never hated them before." Theresa crossed her arms in the door and stared at Lorraine. "What's so different now?"

"I've always hated them." Lorraine closed the drawer and

started searching in the other one. "I just went because you wanted to. They make me sick with all their prancing and phoniness. They're nothing but a couple of fags."

"And we're just a couple of dykes." She spit the words into the air.

Lorraine started as if she'd been slapped. "That's a filthy thing to say, Tee. You can call yourself that if you want to, but I'm not like that. Do you hear me? I'm not!" She slammed the drawer shut.

So she can turn on me but she wouldn't say a word to that scum in the streets, Theresa thought. She narrowed her eyes slowly at Lorraine. "Well, since my friends aren't good enough for the Duchess from Detroit," she said aloud, "I guess you'll go spend another evening with your boyfriend. But I can tell you right now I saw him pass the window just before you came up the block, and he's already stewed to the gills and just singing away. What do you two do down there in that basement—harmonize? It must get kinda boring for you, he only knows one song."

"Well, at least he's not a sarcastic bitch like some people." Theresa looked at Lorraine as if she were a stranger.

"And I'll tell you what we do down there. We talk, Theresa—we really, really talk."

"So you and I don't talk?" Theresa's astonishment was turning into hurt. "After five years, you're going to stand there and say that you can talk to some dried-up wino better than you can to me?"

"You and I don't talk, Tee. You talk—Lorraine listens. You lecture—Lorraine takes notes about how to dress and act and have fun. If I don't see things your way, then you shout—Lorraine cries. You seem to get a kick out of making me feel like a clumsy fool."

"That's unfair, Lorraine, and you know it. I can't count the times I've told you to stop running behind people, sniveling to be their friends while they just hurt you. I've always wanted you to show some guts and be independent."

"That's just it, Tee! You wanted me to be independent of

other people and look to you for the way I should feel about myself, cut myself off from the world, and join you in some crazy idea about being different. When I'm with Ben, I don't feel any different from anybody else in the world."

"Then he's doing you an injustice," Theresa snapped, "because we are different. And the sooner you learn that, the better off you'll be."

"See, there you go again. Tee the teacher and Lorraine the student, who just can't get the lesson right. Lorraine, who just wants to be a human being—a lousy human being who's somebody's daughter or somebody's friend or even somebody's enemy. But they make me feel like a freak out there, and you try to make me feel like one in here. That only place I've found some peace, Tee, is in that damp ugly basement, where I'm not different."

"Lorraine." Theresa shook her head slowly. "You're a lesbian—do you understand that word?—a butch, a dyke, a lesbo, all those things that kid was shouting. Yes, I heard him! And you can run in all the basements in the world, and it won't change that, so why don't you accept it?"

"I have accepted it!" Lorraine shouted. "I've accepted it all my life, and it's nothing I'm ashamed of. I lost a father because I refused to be ashamed of it—but it doesn't make me any *different* from anyone else in the world."

"It makes you damned different!"

"No!" She jerked open the bottom drawer of her dresser and took out a handful of her underwear. "Do you see this? There are two things that have been a constant in my life since I was sixteen years old—beige bras and oatmeal. The day before I first fell in love with a woman, I got up, had oatmeal for breakfast, put on a beige bra, and went to school. The day after I fell in love with that woman, I got up, had oatmeal for breakfast, and put on a beige bra. I was no different the day before or after that happened, Tee."

"And what did you do when you went to school that next day, Lorraine? Did you stand around the gym locker and swap stories with the other girls about this new love in your life, huh? While they were bragging about their boyfriends and the fifty dozen ways they had lost their virginity, did you jump in and say, 'Oh, but you should have seen the one I gave it up to last night?' Huh? Did you? Did you?"

Theresa was standing in front of her and shouting. She saw Lorraine's face crumple, but she still kept pushing her.

"You with your beige bras and oatmeal!" She grabbed the clothes from Lorraine's hand and shook them at her. "Why didn't you stand in that locker room and pass around a picture of this great love in your life? Why didn't you take her to the senior prom? Huh? Why? Answer me!"

"Because they wouldn't have understood," Lorraine whispered, and her shoulders hunched over.

"That's right! There go your precious 'theys' again. They wouldn't understand—not in Detroit, not on Brewster Place, not anywhere! And as long as they own the whole damn world, it's them and us, Sister—them and us. And that spells different!"

Lorraine sat down on the bed with her head in her hands, and heavy spasms shook her shoulders and slender back. Theresa stood over her and clenched her hands to keep herself from reaching out and comforting her. Let her cry. She had to smarten up. She couldn't spend the rest of her life in basements, talking to winos and building cardboard worlds that were just going to come crashing down around her ears.

Theresa left the bedroom and sat in the chair by the living room window. She watched the autumn sky darken and evening crystallize over the tops of the buildings while she sat there with the smugness of those who could amply justify their methods by the proof of their victorious ends. But even after seven cigarettes, she couldn't expel the sour taste in her mouth. She heard Lorraine move around in the bedroom and then go into the shower. She finally joined her in the living room, freshly clothed. She had been almost successful in covering the puffiness around her eyes with makeup.

"I'm ready to go to the party. Shouldn't you start getting dressed?"

Theresa looked at the black pumps and the green dress with black print. Something about the way it hung off of Lorraine's body made her feel guilty.

"I've changed my mind. I don't feel up to it tonight." She turned her head back toward the evening sky, as if the answer to their tangled lives lay in its dark face.

"Then I'm going without you." The tone of Lorraine's voice pulled her face unwillingly from the window.

"You won't last ten minutes there alone, so why don't you just sit down and stop it."

"I have to go, Tee." The urgency in her words startled Theresa, and she made a poor attempt of hiding it.

"If I can't walk out of this house without you tonight, there'll be nothing left in me to love you. And I'm trying, Theresa; I'm trying so hard to hold on to that."

Theresa would live to be a very old woman and would replay those words in her mind a thousand times and then invent a thousand different things she could have said or done to keep the tall yellow woman in the green and black dress from walking out of that door for the last time in her life. But tonight she was a young woman and still in search of answers, and she made the fatal mistake that many young women do of believing that what never existed was just cleverly hidden beyond her reach. So Theresa said nothing to Lorraine that night, because she had already sadly turned her face back to the evening sky in a mute appeal for guidance.

Lorraine left the smoky and noisy club and decided to walk home to stretch the time. She had been ready to leave from the moment she had arrived, especially after she saw the disappointment on everyone's face when she came in without Theresa. Theresa was the one who loved to dance and joke and banter with them and could keep a party going. Lorraine sat in a corner, holding one drink all night and looking so intimidated by the people who approached her that she killed even the most persistent attempts at conversation. She sensed a mood of quiet hysteria and self-mockery in that club, and she fled from it, refusing to see any possible connection with her own existence.

She had stuck it out for an hour, but that wasn't long enough. Tee would still be up, probably waiting at that window, so certain that she would be returning soon. She thought about taking a bus downtown to a movie, but she really didn't want to be alone. If she only had some friends in this city. It was then that she thought about Ben. She could come up the street in back of Brewster Place and cut through the alley to his apartment. Even if Tee was still in that window, she couldn't see that far down the block. She would just tap lightly on his door, and if he wasn't too drunk to hear her, then he wouldn't be too far gone to listen tonight. And she had such a need to talk to someone, it ached within her.

Lorraine smelled the claw-edged sweetness of the marijuana in the shadowy alley before she had gone more than fifty feet in. She stopped and peered through the leaden darkness toward the end and saw no one. She took a few more cautious steps and stopped to look again. There was still no one. She knew she would never reach Brewster like this; each time she stopped her senseless fears would multiply, until it would be impossible to get through them to the other side. There was no one there, and she would just have to walk through quickly to prove this to her pounding heart.

When she heard the first pair of soft thuds behind her, she willed herself not to stop and look back because there was no one there. Another thud and she started walking a little faster to reassure herself of this. The fourth thud started her to running, and then a dark body that had been pressed against the shadowy building swung into her path so suddenly she couldn't stop in time, and she bumped into it and bounced back a few inches.

"Can't you say excuse me, dyke?" C. C. Baker snarled into her face.

Lorraine saw a pair of suede sneakers flying down behind the face in front of hers and they hit the cement with a dead thump. Her bladder began to loosen, and bile worked its way up into her tightening throat as she realized what she must have heard before. They had been hiding up on the wall, watching her come up that back street, and they had waited. The face pushed itself so close to hers that she could look into the flared nostrils and smell the decomposing food caught in its teeth.

"Ain't you got no manners? Stepping on my foot and not saying you sorry?"

She slowly backed away from the advancing face, her throat working convulsively. She turned to run in the direction of the formless thuds behind her. She hadn't really seen them so they weren't there. The four bodies that now linked themselves across the alley hit her conscious mind like a fist, and she cried out, startled. A hand shot itself around her mouth, and her neck was jerked back while a hoarse voice whispered in her ear.

"You ain't got nothing to say now, huh? Thought you was real funny laughing at me in the streets today? Let's see if you gonna laugh now, dyke!" C. C. forced her down on her knees while the other five boys began to close in silently.

She had stepped into the thin strip of earth that they claimed as their own. Bound by the last building on Brewster and a brick wall, they reigned in that unlit alley like dwarfed warrior-kings. Born with the appendages of power, circumcised by a guillotine, and baptized with the steam from a million nonreflective mirrors, these young men wouldn't be called upon to thrust a bayonet into an Asian farmer, target a torpedo, scatter their iron seed from a B-52 into the wound of the earth, point a finger to move a nation, or stick a pole into the moon—and they knew it. They only had that three-hundred-foot alley to serve them as stateroom, armored tank, and executioner's chamber. So Lorraine found herself, on her knees, surrounded by the most dangerous species in existence—human males with an erection to validate in a world that was only six feet wide.

"I'm gonna show you somethin' I bet you never seen before." C. C. took the back of her head, pressed it into the crotch of his jeans, and jerkily rubbed it back and forth while his friends laughed. "Yeah, now don't that feel good? See, that's what you need. Bet after we get through with you, you ain't never gonna wanna kiss no more pussy."

He slammed his kneecap into her spine and her body arched up, causing his nails to cut into the side of her mouth to stifle her cry. He pushed her arched body down onto the cement. Two of the boys pinned her arms, two wrenched open her legs, while C. C. knelt between them and pushed up her dress and tore at the top of her pantyhose. Lorraine's body was twisting in convulsions of fear that they mistook for resistance, and C. C. brought his fist down into her stomach.

"Better lay the fuck still, cunt, or I'll rip open your guts."

The impact of his fist forced air into her constricted throat, and she worked her sore mouth, trying to form the one word that had been clawing inside of her—"Please." It squeezed through her paralyzed vocal cords and fell lifelessly at their feet. Lorraine clamped her eyes shut and, using all of the strength left within her, willed it to rise again.

"Please."

The sixth boy took a dirty paper bag lying on the ground and stuffed it into her mouth. She felt a weight drop on her spread body. Then she opened her eyes and they screamed and screamed into the face above hers—the face that was pushing this tearing pain inside of her body. The screams tried to break through her corneas out into the air, but the tough rubbery flesh sent them vibrating back into her brain, first shaking lifeless the cells that nurtured her memory. Then the cells went that contained her powers of taste and smell. The last that were screamed to death were those that supplied her with the ability to love—or hate.

Lorraine was no longer conscious of the pain in her spine or stomach. She couldn't feel the skin that was rubbing off of her arms from being pressed against the rough cement. What was left of her mind was centered around the pounding motion that was ripping her insides apart. She couldn't tell when they changed places and the second weight, then the third and fourth, dropped on her—it was all one continuous hacksawing of torment that kept her eyes screaming the only word she was fated to utter again and again for the rest of her life. Please.

Her thighs and stomach had become so slimy from her blood and their semen that the last two boys didn't want to touch her, so they turned her over, propped her head and shoulders against the wall, and took her from behind. When they had finished and stopped holding her up, her body fell over like an unstringed puppet. She didn't feel her split rectum or the patches in her skull where her hair had been torn off by grating against the bricks. Lorraine lay in that alley only screaming at the moving pain inside of her that refused to come to rest.

"Hey, C. C., what if she remembers that it was us?"

"Man, how she gonna prove it? Your dick ain't got no fingerprints." They laughed and stepped over her and ran out of the alley.

Lorraine lay pushed up against the wall on the cold ground with her eyes staring straight up into the sky. When the sun began to warm the air and the horizon brightened, she still lay there, her mouth crammed with paper bag, her dress pushed up under her breasts, her bloody pantyhose hanging from her thighs. She would have stayed there forever and have simply died from starvation or exposure if nothing around her had moved. There was no wind that morning, so the tin cans, soda bottles, and loose papers were still. There wasn't even a stray cat or dog rummaging in the garbage cans for scraps. There was nothing moving that early October morning—except Ben.

Ben had come out of the basement and was sitting in his usual place on an old garbage can he had pushed up against the wall. And he was singing and swaying while taking small sips from the pint bottle he kept in his back pocket. Lorraine looked up the alley and saw the movement by the wall. Side to side. Side to side. Almost in perfect unison with the sawing pain that kept moving inside of her. She crept up on her knees, making small grunting sounds like a wounded animal. As she crawled along the alley, her hand brushed a loose brick, and she clawed her fingers around it and dragged it along the ground toward the movement on Brewster Place. Side to side. Side to side.

Mattie left her bed, went to the bathroom, and then put on her tea kettle. She always got up early, for no reason other than habit. The timing mechanism that had been embedded in her on the farm wasn't aware that she now lived in a city. While her coffee water was heating up, she filled a pitcher to water her plants. When she leaned over the plants at the side of the apartment, she saw the body crawling up the alley. She raised the window and leaned out just to be sure the morning light wasn't playing tricks with her eyes. "Merciful Jesus!" She threw a coat over her nightgown, slipped on a pair of shoes, and tried to make her arthritic legs hurry down the steps.

Lorraine was getting closer to the movement. She raised herself up on her bruised and stiffened knees, and the paper bag fell out of her mouth. She supported herself by sliding against the wall, limping up the alley toward the movement while clawing her brick and mouthing her silent word. Side to side. Side to side. Lorraine finally reached the motion on top of the garbage can. Ben slowly started to focus her through his burgundy fog, and just as he opened his lips to voice the words that had formed in his brain—"My God, child, what happened to you?"—the brick smashed down into his mouth. His teeth crumbled into his throat and his body swung back against the wall. Lorraine brought the brick down again to stop the moving head, and blood shot out of his ears, splattering against the can and bottom of the wall. Mattie's screams went ricocheting in Lorraine's head, and she joined them with her own as she brought the brick down again, splitting his forehead and crushing his temple, rendering his brains just a bit more useless than hers were now.

Arms grabbed her around the waist, and the brick was knocked from her hand. The movement was everywhere. Lorraine screamed and clawed at the motions that were running and shouting from every direction in the universe. A tall yellow woman in a bloody green and black dress, scraping at the air, crying, "Please. Please."

THE BLOCK
PARTY

Rain. It began the afternoon of Ben's death and came down day and night for an entire week, so Brewster Place wasn't able to congregate around the wall and keep up a requiem of the whys and hows of his dying. They were forced to exchange opinions among only two or three of themselves at a time, and the closest they could get to the wall was in the front-room windows of the apartments that faced the street. They were confined to their homes and their own thoughts as it became increasingly difficult to tell a night sky from a day sky behind the smoky black clouds. The rains became the heaviest after dusk; water snaked down the gray bricks and flowed into the clogged gutters under sulfurous street lights like a thick dark liquid. Greasy cooking odors seeped into the damp apartment walls; cakes wouldn't rise, and bed sheets remained clammy and cold. Children became listless, and men stayed away longer at night or came in and picked arguments to give themselves a reason they could understand for needing to go out again. The corner bar did a record business that week, and electric bills rose sharply as portable heaters, televisions, and lamps stayed on night and day as Brewster Place tried desperately to bring any kind of warmth and light into their world. By midweek, hopes for the block party started to disappear, the weeks of planning washed through the rusted drains with the gutters' debris.

Although only a few admitted it, every woman on Brewster Place had dreamed that rainy week of the tall yellow woman in the bloody green and black dress. She had come

to them in the midst of the cold sweat of a nightmare, or had
hung around the edges of fitful sleep. Little girls woke up
screaming, unable to be comforted by bewildered mothers
who knew, and yet didn't know, the reason for their daughters' stolen sleep. The women began to grow jumpy and mo-
rose, and the more superstitious began to look upon the rains
as some sort of sign, but they feared asking how or why and
put open Bibles near their bed at night to keep the answers
from creeping upon them in the dark. Even Mattie's sleep
was fitful, her dreams troubling.   . .

"Miss Johnson, you wanna dance?" A handsome teenager
posed himself in a seductive dare before Etta. She ran her
hand down the side of her hair and took off her apron.

"Don't mind if I do." And she pranced around the table.

"Woman, come back here and act your age." Mattie
speared a rib off the grill.

"I am acting it—thirty-five!"

"Umph, you got *regrets* older than that."

The boy spun Etta around under his arms. "Careful, now,
honey. It's still in working order, but I gotta keep it running
in a little lower gear." She winked at Mattie and danced
toward the center of the street.

Mattie shook her head. "Lord, keep her safe, since you
can't keep her sane." She smiled and patted her foot under
the table to the beat of the music while she looked down the
street and inhaled the hope that was bouncing off swinging
hips, sauce-covered fingers, and grinning mouths.

A thin brown-skinned woman, carrying a trench coat and
overnight case, was making her way slowly up the block. She
stopped at intervals to turn and answer the people who called
to her—"Hey, Ciel! Good to see you, girl!"

Ciel—a knot formed at the base of Mattie's heart, and she
caught her breath. "No."

Ciel came up to Mattie and stood in front of her timidly.

"Hi, Mattie. It's been a long time."

"No." Mattie shook her head slowly.

"I know you're probably mad at me. I should have written or at least called before now."

"Child." Mattie placed a hand gently on the side of Ciel's face.

"But I thought about you all the time, really, Mattie."

"Child." Both of Mattie's hands cupped Ciel's face.

"I had to get away; you know that. I needed to leave Brewster Place as far behind me as I could. I just kept going and going until the highway ran out. And when I looked up, I was in San Francisco and there was nothing but an ocean in front of me, and since I couldn't swim, I stayed."

"Child. Child." Mattie pulled Ciel toward her.

"It was awful not to write—I know that." Ciel was starting to cry. "But I kept saying one day when I've gotten rid of the scars, when I'm really well and over all that's happened so that she can be proud of me, then I'll write and let her know."

"Child. Child. Child." Mattie pressed Ciel into her full bosom and rocked her slowly.

"But that day never came, Mattie." Ciel's tears fell on Mattie's chest as she hugged the woman. "And I stopped believing that it ever would."

"Thank God, you found that out." Mattie released Ciel and squeezed her shoulders. "Or I woulda had to wait till the Judgment Day for this here joy."

She gave Ciel a paper napkin to blow her nose. "San Francisco, you said? My, that's a long way. Bet you ain't had none of this out there." She cut Ciel a huge slice of the angel food cake on her table.

"Oh, Mattie, this looks good." She took a bite. "Tastes just like the kind my grandmother used to make."

"It should—it's her recipe. The first night I came to Miss Eva's house she gave me a piece of that cake. I never knew till then why they called it angel food—took one bite and thought I had died and gone to heaven."

Ciel laughed. "Yeah, Grandma could cook. We really had some good times in that house. I remember how Basil and I used to fight. I would go to bed at night and pray. God, please bless Grandma and Mattie, but only bless Basil if he stops breaking my crayons. Do you ever hear from him, Mattie?"

Mattie frowned and turned to baste her ribs. "Naw, Ciel. Guess he ain't been as lucky as you yet. Ain't run out of highway to stop and make him think."

Etta came back to the table out of breath. "Well, looka you!" She grabbed Ciel and kissed her. "Gal, you looking good. Where you been hiding yourself?"

"I live in San Francisco now, Miss Etta, and I'm working in an insurance company."

"Frisco, yeah, that's a nice city—been through there once. But don't tell me it's salt water putting a shine on that face." She patted Ciel on the cheeks. "Bet you got a new fella."

Ciel blushed. "Well, I have met someone and we're sort of thinking about marriage." She looked up at Mattie. "I'm ready to start another family now."

"Lord be praised!" Mattie beamed.

"But he's not black." She glanced hesitantly between Etta and Mattie.

"And I bet he's *not* eight feet tall, and he's *not* as pretty as Billy Dee Williams, and he's *not* president of Yugoslavia, either," Etta said. "You know, we get so caught up with what a man *isn't*. It's what he is that counts. Is he good to you, child?"

"And is he good for you?" Mattie added gently.

"Very much so." Ciel smiled.

"Then, I'm baking your wedding cake." Mattie grinned.

"And I'll come dance at your reception." Etta popped her fingers.

Mattie turned to Etta. "Woman, ain't you done enough dancing today for a lifetime?"

"Aw, hush your mouth. Ciel, will you tell this woman that

this here is a party and you supposed to be having a good time."

"And will you tell that woman," Mattie said, "that hip-shaking is for young folks, and old bags like us is supposed to be behind these tables selling food."

"You two will never change." Ciel laughed.

"Ain't it lucky you got your vacation around this time?" Etta said, tying her apron back on. "Woulda been a shame if you had missed the party."

"No, I'm not on vacation." Ciel looked around slowly. "You know, it was the strangest thing. It rained all last week, and then one night I had a dream about this street, and something just told me I should be here today. So I took a few days off and came—just on an impulse. Funny, huh?"

Mattie and Etta willed themselves not to look at each other.

"What kind of dream, Ciel?" Mattie gripped the basting brush she was holding.

"Oh, I don't know, one of those crazy things that get all mixed up in your head. Something about that wall and Ben. And there was a woman who was supposed to be me, I guess. She didn't look exactly like me, but inside I felt it was me. You know how silly dreams are."

Etta fingered the money in her apron pocket. "What did the woman look like?"

Ciel shrugged her shoulders. "I don't know, like me I guess—tall, skinny." She frowned for a moment. "But she was light-skinned and her hair was different—yes, longer, but pinned up somehow." She looked at Etta as the words began to leave her mouth with a will of their own. "And she had on a green dress with like black trimming, and there were red designs or red flowers or something on the front." Ciel's eyes began to cloud. "And something bad had happened to me by the wall—I mean to her—something bad had happened to her. And Ben was in it somehow." She stared at the wall and shuddered. "Ah, who knows? It was just a crazy dream, that's all."

She smiled at Etta and Mattie, but something in their faces stifled it. "Why are you looking at me like that? What's wrong?"

Mattie became intent on basting her ribs, and Etta answered, "Nothing, honey. I was just trying to figure out what number I could play off your dream. Now, I know snakes is 436 and a blue Cadillac is 224, but I gotta look in my book to see what a wall is. What do ya play off a wall, Mattie?"

Mattie kept looking down at the grill. "Woman, you know I don't bother with that foolishness. If I wanna throw my money away, I can just toss it out the window. Don't have to give it to no number runner. Ciel, these ribs are ready now. You want a sandwich 'fore they all gone? These folks are eating up a storm today."

"Not right now, that cake filled me up." She looked around the street and snapped her fingers. "Now I know what's missing—where's old Ben? Downstairs sleeping off a hangover?"

Mattie suddenly decided that her meat still needed more basting, and she busied her eyes looking for the sauce. "Honey, Ben died last Saturday."

"Oh, I'm sorry to hear that. The wine must have finally got him."

"You might say that." Etta's jaws were tight.

The music and noise dimmed in Mattie's ears, and she saw the sliding and twisting bodies beating at the air in a dull vacuum. Teeth were tearing into meat and throats were draining the liquid from aluminum cans while children ran wildly among the crowds, forming muted screams and kicking aside loose paper and empty bottles. Dark faces distorted into masks of pleasure, surprise, purpose, and satisfaction—thin masks that were glued on by the warm air of the October sun.

"Oh, God," Mattie begged silently, looking up at the sky, "please don't let it rain." She saw out of the corner of her eye that Etta was also looking toward the heavens with an expression on her face that was the closest to prayer Mattie had ever seen on her friend.

A red and yellow beach ball flew into the middle of Mattie's grill, and the noises of the street rushed back in on her. "Mercy!" She snatched the ball from the rack before it melted over the coals.

"Sorry, Mattie." Kiswana ran up to the table. "I was playing with Brucie and he threw it too far."

"That's all right, child. Just didn't think anyone was gonna want barbecued rubber."

Kiswana took the ball and went back to Cora Lee's stoop.

"See what I told ya?" Cora said, sitting on the steps with her hands resting on her protruding stomach. "He can't do nothing right." She called to Bruce, "Now come on over here and sit down. No more ball for you."

"I don't wanna sit down. I wanna piece of cake."

"I ain't got no more money for cake."

"You got Dorian a piece of cake—I wanna piece of cake!" Bruce started kicking on the stoop railing.

"That's right, break your foot. You weren't happy enough breaking your arm—now you wanna break your foot."

"I'll buy him a piece," Kiswana offered.

"No, he's already had one. And if he don't get away from here, he's not gonna have any teeth left to eat nothin' with!" Cora made an attempt to lift herself off the stoop.

"You ole big belly!" Bruce yelled and ran up the street.

Cora sat back down with a sigh. "Miserable. Just plain miserable. You think they take any pity on me being in this condition? Not one bit. They almost drove me crazy last week and with all that rain I couldn't send 'em outside. And I never got a minute's sleep. When you pregnant you can't sleep good at night—kept having all kinds of weird dreams."

"I know." Kiswana nodded. "I hoped it would stop raining for the party today. Isn't it great? You know, we've already collected over a hundred dollars."

"That much?" a woman nearby asked.

"Guess after we get a lawyer and haul that landlord's butt in court, he'll be more than willing to give us some heat this year," another one said.

"Imagine, he only delivered oil twice all last winter."

"I know," Cora said. "Had to keep my oven burning and my gas bill was something ridiculous."

"Guess he figure niggers don't need no heat."

"Yeah, we supposed to be from Africa, anyway. And it's so hot over there them folks don't know what oil is."

Everybody laughed but Kiswana. "You know, that's not really true. It snows in some parts of Africa, and Nigeria is one of the most important exporters of oil in the world."

The women stopped laughing and looked at her as you would at someone who had totally missed the point of a joke that should need no explanation.

Theresa came out of the next building and put some boxes on top of the garbage cans and went back inside.

"I thought she had moved already," someone whispered.

"No, I think she's leaving today."

An uneasy quiet fell over all the women on the stoop.

"So how much more we need 'fore we have enough for a lawyer?" Cora Lee asked Kiswana.

"Huh?" Kiswana had been staring at the wall, as if trying to remember something important that had escaped her. "Oh, well, maybe another hundred or so. But that won't be a problem at the rate we're going." She looked up quickly at the sky. "As long as the weather doesn't break."

"Yeah," the mothers mumbled.

"Better get back out here and help sell some more stuff."

"Yeah, I got more ice cubes up in the freezer. Folks don't wanna buy warm sodas."

"Anybody see Sonya?" Cora Lee suddenly realized that her baby was gone. She pulled her bulky body up from the steps. "Lord, it was the worst day of my life when that girl started walking." She began moving through the crowds calling to her. "Sonya! Sonya!"

Kiswana sighed. "Guess I should go around and collect some more money."

A cloud had almost completely covered the thin strip of blue sky that lay between the two sets of buildings, and a cold wind started pulling at the thin strings on the balloons and uncurling the crepe paper entwined on the stoop railings. The colors on Brewster Place had dissolved into one mass of leaden gray that matched the bricks of the buildings. The crowd was rapidly thinning out as people from the neighboring streets gathered their children and began hurrying toward home.

Kiswana went over to one of the tables. "I guess we better start clearing up—it's going to rain."

The woman had just taken the plastic wrap from around a fresh coconut cake. "It ain't gonna rain," she said, and started slicing the cake and putting it on paper plates.

"Don't do that—it'll get wet! You can save it for later."

The woman looked straight into Kiswana's eyes with the knife poised in the middle of the cake. "It ain't gonna rain." And she brought the knife down with a whack that made the girl jump, and she backed away.

The large rectangular speakers were still flinging music out into the street, but the heavy air was weighing in against them and muffling the sound. The only people who were dancing were those who lived on Brewster Place. They didn't look up at the rapidly darkening sky or stop moving when static would override the music. They danced from memory, until the measured beat caught up with them again.

Kiswana darted among the dancers and went to the boy playing the records. "You better unhook your stereo before the rain ruins it."

"People are still dancing."

"I know they're still dancing," she cried. "But it's going to rain soon!"

The dark clouds had knotted themselves into a thick smoky fist, and the wind was so strong now that it blew her braids into her face.

"I have to keep playing if people wanna dance." The boy reached for another album.

Kiswana pushed her hair out of her eyes. "This is insane!" And she ran to Mattie's table.

"Don't bother with that chicken now." A man from another street was saying, "I better be getting home. Don't wanna get caught in a downpour."

Etta kept wrapping the sandwich. "Look, this here is a party to help our block. Now you asked for this sandwich, and you gonna stand here and eat it!"

"Lady, look, I'll give you the dollar, but I'm not gonna catch pneumonia out here " He put the dollar on the table and started walking away.

"No, wait. You don't have to pay. Just stay here and eat it—please!"

He threw her a puzzled look over his shoulder and almost ran down the street.

"Ain't he a fool?" she said to Kiswana and angrily threw the chicken sandwich on the table.

Kiswana slowly edged away from Etta and, her heart pounding, she turned toward Mattie.

"Mattie, it's going to rain," she pleaded. "Please, we've got to get the money collected. We've got to . . ." And her voice dissolved into tears.

"Now, don't fret yourself, child." Mattie seemed to be rearranging the ribs on the grill in slow motion. "See, you're a city girl. Where I come from we know clouds don't always mean rain—ain't it so, Etta?"

"Sure is. Many a day I was working in my daddy's fields and would spot a cloud and pray for it to send some rain so I could rest. And nine times out of ten I prayed in vain."

They both turned toward Kiswana and smiled. It seemed to take an eternity for her to shake her head at them, and she numbly appealed to the young woman in the trench coat who was standing beside them.

"It's going to rain." The tears were streaking Kiswana's face.

"I know," Ciel whispered, and she pulled her coat tightly around her and looked slowly up and down the street at the wilting crepe paper hanging from broken stoop railings and the loosened balloons climbing up the building fronts past rotting windowsills and corroded fire escapes. When her eyes had come full circle to the sagging brick wall, she shuddered, "Oh, God, I know."

The first light misting of the wind hit Kiswana on her arms as Cora Lee melted in front of them.

"Sonya! Anybody seen Sonya?"

The little girl was crouching in front of the wall, scraping at the base with a smudged Popsicle stick. Cora's swollen body flowed toward the child.

"I been looking all over for you—put that down! I ain't got enough worries without you playing with filth in the streets." She bent over to snatch up the child and spank her hand.

A heavy drop of water hit Kiswana's face like a cold wad of spit.

Cora pulled Sonya's hand away from the wall and uncovered a dark stain on the edge of the brick that the child had been scraping. The stain began to widen and deepen.

"Blood—there's still blood on this wall," Cora whispered, and dropped to her knees. She took the Popsicle stick and started digging around the loose mortar near the brick. "It ain't right; it just ain't right. It shouldn't still be here." The fragile stick splintered so she used her fingernails, the gravelly cement lacerating her knuckles. "Blood ain't got no right still being here."

As she yanked the brick out, the boy who had been playing the stereo ran past her with one of his speakers in his arms; two more men hurried behind, carrying the other sections. Another man grabbed Sonya up and took her under the eaves of the building. All of the men and children now stood huddled in the doorways. Cora ran to Mattie's table and held out the brick.

"Oh, Miss Mattie—look! There's still blood on that wall!"

"Oh, God," Mattie said as she watched the rain splattering

on the hot charcoal, sending steam up through the iron grill. She saw it drumming down on their backs and shoulders, blowing into their faces and up their nostrils, soaking the paper tablecloths, and turning cakes and pies into a sodden mass of crumbs and fruit.

"Get that thing out of here!" She grabbed the brick and gave it to Etta, who took it over to the next table. And it was passed by the women from hand to hand, table to table, until the brick flew out of Brewster Place and went spinning out onto the avenue.

Mattie grabbed Cora by the arm. "Come on, let's make sure that's the only one."

They ran back to the wall and started prying at another stained brick, Mattie digging into the crumbling mortar with her barbecue fork. She finally got it out and threw it behind her. Etta picked it up and began passing it down the street.

"This one's got it, too!" Cora started tearing at another brick.

"We gonna need some help here," Mattie called out. "It's spreading all over!"

Women flung themselves against the wall, chipping away at it with knives, plastic forks, spiked shoe heels, and even bare hands; the water pouring under their chins, plastering their blouses and dresses against their breasts and into the cracks of their hips. The bricks piled up behind them and were snatched and relayed out of Brewster Place past overturned tables, scattered coins, and crushed wads of dollar bills. They came back with chairs and barbecue grills and smashed them into the wall. The "Today Brewster—Tomorrow America" banner had been beaten into long strands of red and gold that clung to the wet arms and faces of the women.

Ciel's coat had blown open, and muddy clay streaked the front of her blouse. She tried to pass a brick to Kiswana, who looked as if she had stepped into a nightmare.

"There's no blood on those bricks!" Kiswana grabbed Ciel by the arm. "You know there's no blood—it's raining. It's just raining!"

Ciel pressed the brick into Kiswana's hand and forced her fingers to curl around it. "Does it matter? Does it really matter?"

Kiswana looked down at the wet stone and her rain-soaked braids leaked onto the surface, spreading the dark stain. She wept and ran to throw the brick spotted with her blood out into the avenue.

Cars were screeching and sliding around the flying bricks that came out of Brewster. The side window of a station wagon exploded into a webbed mass of glass and it skidded into the back of a black Datsun, pushing it off the street into a telephone pole.

Theresa came out of her building with a suitcase in her hand.

"Over here!" A cab pulled up and she opened the back door. "I have another bag in the house—I couldn't carry it with the umbrella. Wait a minute."

"Lady, are you crazy? There's a riot on this street!" And the driver sped off, a brick just missing his hubcap.

"Son-of-a-bitch!" she called behind the cab. "You still have my suitcase in that car!"

She turned and looked down the street. The women had started dragging furniture out of their apartments, shattering it against the wall.

"Dumb bastard, they're only having a lousy block party. And they didn't invite me."

Cora Lee came panting up with a handful of bricks, her stomach heaving and almost visible under her soaked dress.

"Here, please, take these. I'm so tired."

Theresa turned her back on her.

"Please. Please." Cora held out the stained bricks.

"Don't say that!" Theresa screamed. "Don't ever say that!" She grabbed the bricks from Cora and threw one into the avenue, and it burst into a cloud of green smoke.

"Now, you go back up there and bring me some more, but don't ever say that again—to anyone!"

The blunt-edged whoop of the police sirens could be heard ramming through the traffic on its way to Brewster Place. Theresa flung her umbrella away so she could have both hands free to help the other women who were now bringing her bricks. Suddenly, the rain exploded around their feet in a fresh downpour, and the cold waters beat on the top of their heads—almost in perfect unison with the beating of their hearts.

Mattie turned over in bed, the perspiration running down her chest, gluing her nightgown to her arms and back. She brought her hand up to her sweating forehead and wondered why it was so hot in the room.

Forcing her eyes to open, she saw that the sun had finally come out, but her electric heater was still set on high.

"Lord, be praised. I ain't gonna need this today." She turned the heater off and went to her front-room window and pulled up the shades.

After a week of continuous rain Brewster Place was now bathed in a deluge of sunlight. People were already out in the street setting up. Long crinkled strands of crepe paper were being unrolled and balloons were being tied to the stoop railings. Kiswana was taping her banner up on the wall and the gold lettering glowed so brightly in the sun, it was almost painful to look at.

"It's just like a miracle," Mattie opened her window, "to think it stopped raining today of all days."

The sun was shining on everything: Kiswana's gold earrings, the broken glass out on the avenue, the municipal buildings downtown—even on the stormy clouds that had formed on the horizon and were silently moving toward Brewster Place.

Etta came out on the stoop and looked up at Mattie in the window.

"Woman, you still in bed? Don't you know what day it is? We're gonna have a party."

DUSK

No one cries when a street dies. There's no line of mourners to walk behind the coffin wheeled on the axis of the earth and lidded by the sky. No organ-piped dirges, no whispered prayers, no eulogy. No one is there when a street dies. It isn't dead when the last door is locked, and the last pair of footsteps echo up the sidewalk, reluctant to turn the corner and melt into another reality. It dies when the odors of hope, despair, lust, and caring are wiped out by the seasonal winds; when dust has settled into the cracks and scars, leveling their depths and discolorations—their reasons for being; when the spirit is trapped and fading in someone's memory. So when Brewster dies, it will die alone.

It watched its last generation of children torn away from it by court orders and eviction notices, and it had become too tired and sick to help them. Those who had spawned Brewster Place, countless twilights ago, now mandated that it was to be condemned. With no heat or electricity, the water pipes froze in the winter, and arthritic cold would not leave the buildings until well into the spring. Hallways were blind holes, and plaster crumbled into snaggled gaps. Vermin bred in uncollected garbage and spread through the walls. Brewster had given what it could—all it could—to its "Afric" children, and there was just no more. So it had to watch, dying but not dead, as they packed up the remnants of their dreams and left—some to the arms of a world that they would have to pry open to take them, most to inherit another aging street and the privilege of clinging to its decay.

And Brewster Place is abandoned, the living smells worn thin by seasons of winds, the grime and dirt blanketing it in an anonymous shroud. Only waiting for death, which is a second behind the expiration of its spirit in the minds of its children. But the colored daughters of Brewster, spread over the canvas of time, still wake up with their dreams misted on the edge of a yawn. They get up and pin those dreams to wet laundry hung out to dry, they're mixed with a pinch of salt and thrown into pots of soup, and they're diapered around babies. They ebb and flow, ebb and flow, but never disappear. So Brewster Place still waits to die.

Also available
from Methuen Paperbacks

GLORIA NAYLOR

Linden Hills

Linden Hills is a rich, private residential estate in America. Intended as a symbol that blacks can be just like whites, Linden Hills is in fact an infernal place, and as two young blacks, Willie and Lester, odd-job their way down the hill in the week before Christmas, the layers of hypocrisy and self-destruction which are its foundation become exposed.

And at the bottom of the hill waits the estate's sinister owner, Luther Nedeed, feudal baron of the estate and of his own family, whose perpetuation of the cruel, inverted values of Linden Hills must ultimately be confronted.

'A clever, subtle book'   *London Review of Books*

LOUISE MERIWETHER

Daddy was a Number Runner

Francie Coffin, twelve years old, lives in a run-down tenement in Harlem, daughter of a proud father and a God-fearing mother. Darting around the streets of Harlem with the number slips for her father, Francie's manner is tough and resourceful. Yet she is still a child, naive and innocent, and for a time her concerns are the urgent concerns of childhood – avoiding a fight with her best friend Sukie, attracting the attention of Vincent, the boy from out of town.

But Francie's Harlem is a world full of danger – drunks, riots, prostitutes and pimps – and the more she sees the more she understands about her future. Her story is a moving account of a young woman's rite of passage, of the journey from childhood to adulthood and the inescapable knowledge that transition brings.

NAWAL EL SAADAWI

Death of an Ex-Minister

Translated by Shirley Eber

In his mother's arms, a government minister describes an encounter with a junior employee, a woman, who would not lower her eyes in his presence, would not submit. This incident, which shatters his preconceived notions of acceptable behaviour, ultimately leads to his breakdown, dismissal and death.

This cunning tale of how fear of authority, instilled in childhood, becomes authority over those perceived to be weaker – men over women – and blind subserviance towards those perceived to be stronger is the first in this subtle collection by Egypt's leading woman writer. While writing of Arab society, her themes are universal – the meaning of life and love in *A Modern Love Letter*; female sexuality in *The Veil*; repressed emotions in *Masculine Confession*.

Nawal El Saadawi's sympathetic and powerful stories of sexual politics in today's society offer a fresh and moving perception that will touch many readers.

JULIA VOZNESENSKAYA

The Women's Decameron

'Ten women, who ... have all just given birth in a Leningrad clinic, are unexpectedly quarantined together for ten days. Each night each woman undertakes to tell a story on some previously chosen subject: first love, rape, revenge, jealously, money, betrayal, happiness, noble deeds or sex in absurd situations ... It is an intimate world, startingly frank about personal and social relationships and, as such, reveals more about Soviet life than anything to be read in a newspaper.' Sheila MacLeod, *New Statesman*

'Now here is a robust, spicy saga of adultery, jealousy and betrayal ... a sharp and savage review of Soviet life' *Sunday Telegraph*

'Vigorous, funny, appealing and appalling tales' *Books and Booksmen*

'Lively tales about women getting by, even getting some fun, however grim, out of life in the Soviet Union' Hilary Spurling, *Guardian*

'Plain, simple, fine ... useful, important and oddly cheering ... a veritable riot of local colour, a very warm and funny book' *City Limits*

'An extraordinary account of what life is like for modern Russian women' *Literary Review*

'A remarkable book' *London Review of Books*

APHRA BEHN

Oroonoko

Virginia Woolf suggested that, 'All women together ought to let flowers fall upon the tomb of Aphra Behn . . . for it was she who earned them the right to speak their minds.' Certainly, as the first female professional writer, and the author of many novels, prose works, poems, translations and eighteen plays, Aphra Behn (1640–1689) stands securely at the heart of the literary tradition, well before the writers generally considered to have established the novel form.

This volume of novellas and short stories represents the best of Aphra Behn's short fiction. *Oroonoko*, a faction, and the first prose work in English to have a black hero, is remarkable not only as a romantic tale and a terrifying account of contemporary slavery, but also as a political allegory and as a timeless comment on white racism. Other stories confirm Behn's wit, her grasp of politics and ethics and her willingness – in contemporary terms – to write openly about sex.

Selected and introduced by Maureen Duffy, Behn's biographer and a novelist, poet, and contemporary commentator herself, this book gives modern readers an opportunity to reassess a woman of extraordinary talent and possible the most neglected of British literary innovators.

NTOZAKE SHANGE

Betsey Brown

Betsey Brown is a black girl aged thirteen, poised at the still point between the enchanted world of childhood and the passionate promises – romantic and political – of the adult world. The time is 1957, the place is the black community of St Louis, and Betsey's private drama takes place against the cultural unheaval of the school integration programme and the Civil Rights movement.

Into this beguiling portrait of an extended black family confronting racism and court-ordered integration, as well as the stresses within the black community itself, Ntozake Shange weaves a magical story of adolescent awakening. Betsey's impulsive first romance, her impatience to be grown and her intimations of approaching adulthood are counterpointed by her mother's and grandmother's story, and all are combined into one magnificent song of a black family at a specific and decisive point in American history.

Methuen Modern Fiction

While every effort is made to keep prices low, it is sometimes necessary to increase prices at short notice. Methuen Paperbacks reserves the right to show new retail prices on covers which may differ from those previously advertised in the text or elsewhere.

The prices shown below were correct at the time of going to press.

All these books are available at your bookshop or newsagent, or can be ordered direct from the publisher. Just tick the titles you want and fill in the form below.

Methuen Paperbacks, Cash Sales Department, PO Box 11, Falmouth, Cornwall TR10 109EN.

Please send cheque or postal order, no currency, for purchase price quoted and allow the following for postage and packing:

UK   55p for the first book, 22p for the second book and 14p for each additional book ordered to a maximum charge of £1.75.

BFPO and Eire   55p for the first book, 22p for the second book and 14p for each next seven books, thereafter 8p per book.

Overseas   £1.00 for the first book plus 25p per copy for each additional book.
Customers

NAME (Block Letters) ....

ADDRESS...

....